A Candle in the Dark

and other tales

A
Candle
in the
Dark

and other tales

C.L. Phillips

Dedication

This one is for Jenn,

Whose love and kindness

Are soothing balm to my heart,

Whose touch and gentle whispers are

My candle in the dark

Introduction

I find it absurdly difficult to classify my own stories.

There are so many genres of fiction, and numerous sub genres beneath them. Sometimes I know when I set out what type of story I intend to write. Often, what is created during that venture is something unlike what I planned. I do work to build plot and character into one cohesive mechanism, to set forth interesting tales that might mean something in the end. That being said, what should I call my stories? To what genre or genres do they belong?

People ask me what kind of things I write. I wish I could give them solid, satisfying answers. But the truth is I don't know. I really just don't know sometimes. So, I give blanket responses: science fiction, fantasy, horror, and some literary stuff (whatever that means). Those are the categories you will find on my website, cl-phillips.com. There I have posted some free stories for you. But those genre categories are so broad. Science fiction ranges from alien first contact (see *Skittens* in this volume) to time travel to genetic engineering to futuristic and so on. Fantasy includes so much, and much that I don't fully understand though I love it all. From sword and sorcery to epic fantasy, urban fantasy to dark fantasy, I am a fan of everything that involves magic and magical beings. Some of my love for fantasy bleeds into my affinity for horror tales, ranging from the cosmic horror of Lovecraft to slasher flicks and ghost stories. Are ghost stories fantasy or horror? Does it depend on the author's intent, or the reader's perception? Is there a hard and fast rule? Can a ghost story be one or the other? Can it be both? In my previous collection, *Figures in the Forest and other tales*, there is a story called *The Ghost on the Hill*. I really like that story. I would call it horror. If you ask me about it, I will tell you it's a horror story. But is it? Kind of. It's a love story, maybe a couple of love stories. Mostly it's a story of relationships. And if we're honest about it, aren't all the good stories about relationships?

And that brings us to the book you're holding in your hands. At its heart, *A Candle in the Dark and other tales* is a collection of eleven stories that are, at their core, the stories of relationships.

Soldiers bound by blood and battle; a father and son overcoming trauma; a prisoner and her executioners trying to understand one another; cowboys on the range living like a close-knit family; and a man lost in darkness trying to make his way toward the candle left burning for him.

These relationships and more await in the coming pages.

CLP
October 2021

Table of Contents

The Thirsty

Sands, unbroken by mosque or minaret,
Unstruck by tower or battlement;
Sands, endless, unbounded, eternal;
Sands, quivering with reflected heat,
Undulating as waves upon a frozen sea,
Conjoining the sky in a coppered haze
Where monstrous demons, sight-conjured,
Tread reelingly a dance of sun-desire,
Twisting and turning in a burning maze,
Tireless, grotesque, sinister.

Arthur Crew Inman
from *Desert*

The Thirsty

We wandered in that God-forsaken desert for two days. I didn't even know which country we were in now, whether we'd crossed borders. Where were the lines we were fighting over? Where was basecamp? There had been twenty of us when we set out. After the first firefight, we were down to thirteen. A day later, six remained. Now we were three, and we were lost in the blistering heat, choking sand, and frigid nights. We were at the base of a mountain range, stony foothills on one side, the vast, empty desert to the other. If only we could get into those mountains, we could take shelter in a cave, maybe even find water.

When Lieutenant Scott died, the bullets took out the radio and sat phone. We were walking blind now, deaf, dead to the world so far as anyone knew. He had been the ranking officer, I think, after the second wave of death struck us. Didn't seem to matter much now. We were dying from heat and thirst. Hunger was setting in, but it wouldn't kill us. Hell, we'd be dead long before it had a chance to.

By process of elimination, Powell was in command now. I suppose Watts could have argued it if he'd felt like splitting hairs, but the truth is nobody wants to be the man in charge when things go sideways, when a squad falls, and everyone dies. Just as well, anyway, because on the third day of wandering Watts stepped on a mine. It was an old mine, I think, maybe one of the early prototypes from some long-forgotten war, because it didn't kill him outright. Just blew a leg off.

People say "clean off" but this was anything but clean. One moment Watts was a whole man, a walking tank of nearly 250 pounds, humping his gear through the desert, and the next moment he was two very distinct pieces. Here was 200 pounds of screaming agony just a few feet from me, and there, about ten yards out, lay a silent hunk of leg, boot still strapped on, muscles still twitching, the end that was once a hip now a pile of barbecued pulled pork.

Powell went to his knees, pressing his hands to the wounds, staring down at the senseless, screaming face of Mike Watts. "We got you, brother. You're going to be all right."

No, he wasn't. Powell was a mechanic and had some experience with demolitions, but I was a medic. Before enlisting, I'd been a paramedic and was considering a career in medicine. I'd seen some bad wounds that had been healed, seemingly impossible situations that people had survived. But that had been in a city with a hospital, doctors, equipment, sterile rooms, the whole works. We were in a desert, I had no gear, and Mike Watts was about thirty seconds from bleeding out.

"Help him, Duffy." Powell turned his wide sand-colored eyes up to me. It wasn't an order. I don't know what it was. Denial? Hope? Desperation?

I had one morphine tablet left. After a moment's hesitation, I knelt beside Watts and dug the tablet out. "Here, brother. Swallow this."

Watts stared past me, looking up at the purple twilight sky. He was shaking now. Shock was seizing him. When he didn't acknowledge my presence, but continued shrieking, reaching for his phantom leg with convulsing arms, I tried to force the morphine into his mouth.

Something in the sand moved beneath me. I was knocked aside, falling from my knees and onto my face, the morphine tablet falling into the shifting sand. It felt like a tiny, powerful earthquake centered beneath me. Something in the sand pressed against my torso and suddenly I was afraid I'd fallen onto another mine. The pressure nudged me, moved, as if whatever I'd fallen on was alive and was stirring, searching for something. It wasn't a mine. I got to my feet and looked around.

All around us the sand was swirling, rising in man-sized mounds as if some hulking creatures were trying to break through the surface, but could not. They were like ghosts in the twilight, the shifting sand clinging to their forms, hiding their true visages. One would half-rise then plunge low, its body racing through the sand, creating a ridge, leaving a shifting dune in its wake as it darted toward us. Some of them were moving toward Watts's severed leg, others were swimming toward us, sand flying furiously into the air, stinging my eyes, pelting my flesh.

"What the hell is this?" Powell shouted.

"I don't know." And I didn't. How could I?

Watts had quieted as the flow of his blood slowed, his heart winding down to its final beats. He had just enough strength left for a final surge of screams, though, and he released an agonized wail as something latched onto his mangled thigh. From the sand, formed of the sand itself, came a mouth like that of a lamprey. The coarse, convulsing maw latched onto the hip joint. At first, the opening was too small to take in the stump, but as I watched in horror, the sand stretched out, opening like a sinkhole to wrap itself around the bloody stub at Watts's waist.

The long mound of sand, wormlike in shape, began to pulsate slowly, widening slightly in segmented rhythm as it sucked the lifeblood from the withering corpse of Mike Watts. Watts was silent now, his body looking pale and shriveled, as if every last drop of blood had been removed from him. The sand creatures, apparently sated, released Watts's corpse and sunk back into the sand.

"To those rocks," I shouted, spotting a small pile of boulders and stones. It looked like the beginning of a mountain that had changed its mind. There was no way we'd reach the mountains. We couldn't outrun the things beneath the sand. All I could think to do was to get to elevated ground; get off the sand. In my panic, I believed that would save us.

We sprinted to the rocks and climbed up to the highest point, just ten feet above the churning sand. There were similar stacks of stone in the distance, between us and the mountains. They looked like squatting giants in the falling darkness.

Powell raised his rifle and began firing rounds into the myriad shapes of shifting sand. They were all around us, the desert floor moving the way a carcass crawls with the movement of the worms eating it from the inside out. What could I do? Watts couldn't be saved. I took up my own assault rifle and started shooting every mound of sand I could see in the darkening dusk.

The creatures seemed not to notice. More than once my shot struck my mark. I put round after round into the moving ground, but each nimble mound kept moving as if I'd done nothing. Powell was the best shot I knew. He hit more than I did, not that it mattered. The things went about their gruesome business as if oblivious to our presence.

"Stop firing," Powell said. "Better save our rounds."

"You ever seen anything like that?" I asked him.

Powell shook his head. "Nobody has."

"What now?"

"No idea. You?"

I looked at the sky. Stars were appearing one-by-one, blinking carelessly, and watching us like impartial eyes. The mountains were so big and looked so near, but I knew they were a long way off. "If we assume these things only live in the sand, we can assume the mountains are safe."

The Thirsty

"Let's assume nothing is safe, Duffy. We've lost eighteen men in four days. We just lost Watts to something we can't identify." Powell sat down heavily, lay his rifle across his lap, and put his head in his hands.

I shone my flashlight out over the desert. Here was the withered husk of Watts, over there was a thin stick that had been his leg. The sand was still. Nothing stirred. Behind me, a cool breeze came down off the mountain. "They're gone," I said.

Powell raised his head, looked out over the area, following my light beam with his eyes. "We don't know that," he said. "Best to wait here till daylight."

So, we waited. That night, we sat propped against each other, his back to mine, perched atop that big flat rock. We didn't speak. I watched the stars and moon make their way through the sky above that chain of mountain ridges until at last, shivering against the desert night and trembling from a fear I didn't know I possessed, I fell asleep.

~

The sound of distant voices brought me to. Not only voices. I heard sheep and goats up on the mountain. The sun was rising in the distance, casting a strange warm glow over the stretch of desert we'd come across the previous day. Squinting and shielding my eyes, I peered toward the foot of the mountain.

"Wake up, Powell," I said, shifting my weight and letting him tip over. We'd slept sitting up, leaning against one another. "We've got company."

Powell's body jerked rigid. "Where?" His head whipped back and forth, scanning the sand and I caught him staring down at the wasted form of Watts. "I told you they hadn't gone."

"Not that," I said. "On the mountain. Shepherds."

I put my rifle to my shoulder and peered through the scope. An old man led a small herd of sheep and goats through the scrub and sparse grass of a mountain pass. With him, trailing behind with the stragglers, were three younger men. They wore long loose-fitting robes with their heads covered against the rising sun and cloth drawn across their faces against the blowing sand.

They moved down the mountainside and up a long outcropping that reminded me of the mast of a ship the way it seemed to point up toward the sky and out over the barren brown land. The three younger men carried staves or shepherd's crooks. The old man held a gleaming knife.

"What are they doing?" Powell asked.

"I think they mean to kill those animals. Grab your gun. Take a look for yourself."

"No. You watch them. I'll keep my eyes on the ground."

Two of the young men took a sheep by its hind legs, a leg apiece, and held it up over the edge of the cliff. The third wasted no time and clubbed the beast in the head with a single, solid blow from his staff. The moment the sheep was stunned, the old man grabbed it by an ear and plunged the blade into its throat. With a single fluid movement, the blade entered and was pulled away, nearly severing the head.

The Thirsty

A fountain of blood poured over the cliff, raining down onto the sand. I followed the crimson flow with my eye and what I saw terrified me more than the events of the previous night. At the bottom of the cliff were gathered no fewer than a dozen little dust devils. Whirlwinds of sentient sand rose up from the desert floor looking at one moment like something from an old Warner Brothers cartoon, and the next like something demonic. Whatever they were, they seemed self-aware, like dogs sitting up for treats. The whirlwinds swayed and circled, rebounding off one another like bumper cars. But it was the gaping orifices at the top of each whirling funnel that made my blood run cold.

The mouths—if you can call them mouths—pulsed peristaltically like the lips of a nursing baby, each vying for a spot beneath the outpouring of blood that was raining down. As I watched, the first sheep's carcass fell through the air and was caught in one of the wicked whirlwinds. The funnel spun wildly for a moment as it removed all the fluids from the body like a juicer squeezing an orange; then the sheep carcass, as withered and dried as Watts's remains, was spat out like an olive pit.

I moved my scope back to the butchers atop the rock. Another animal had been killed and was in its death throes, kicking violently, its forelegs and head thrashing as the two men held its hind legs tight. They did not toss it over until the blood from its neck stopped flowing.

"You won't believe this," I said. "They're feeding those things."

Powell stepped beside me and looked through his scope. "I'll be damned. Why would they do that?"

"I don't know," I said. "Can you run?"

"Is there a choice?"

"I think we can reach the base of the mountain if we sprint."

"That's got to be four, maybe five hundred yards."

"Don't think about it," I told him. "Just run. Let's go."

I didn't wait for another response. Gripping my rifle tight as I could, I hopped down from the rock, praying that none of those things were in the sand between me and the mountain. My lungs caught fire instantly. I was dehydrated and hungry. My legs were cramping. Yet, I pushed on, putting one foot before the other and digging down deep, running like my life depended on it. It did, of course, or so I believed.

With each shift of sand beneath my feet, each spray of coarse wind in my face, I was certain that the sucking death that had killed Watts was rising up to take me down. But nothing came. Nothing but the mountain and the deep agony rushing through my starved limbs.

At last we came to a small strip of land where sand gave way to stone and small scrub bushes stood in a scattered mass. We'd made it out of the sand. Climbing up onto another large rock, I took Powell's hand and heaved him up. Together we fell back on the warm stone, faces to the lightening sky, our hearts beating hard against the stone. I could hear Powell's pulse pounding in my ears. We lay there a long time, gasping, panting, glad to be alive.

"What now?" I asked once I was able to speak.

"We need to get to those shepherds," Powell said.

"Why? They were sacrificing offerings to those things."

"That means they know what they are," he said. "Those things killed Watts. Whatever they are, they're a powerful secret our military doesn't know about."

"We're doing recon now?"

"We were doing recon before, Duffy. This is a bit different. Nobody's ever reported anything like this. We need to know what we're dealing with."

"I just want to get out of this desert." I sat up and looked back to where the men were still slaughtering their offerings. "Honestly, I don't care what they are. I don't give a shit what kind of messed up religion this is. I just want to get back to base, back to civilization."

"Soon enough," Powell said. "But first we'll have some answers."

~

Methodically, we went from rock to rock, minimizing our time on the sand. We made our way into the low sloping stone paths at the foot of the mountains and up toward the four men and their dwindling supply of sacrificial animals.

"Hang back," Powell said as we came to the base of the high ridge the men stood upon. "We'll wait until they're finished; until those things leave."

"Fine by me," I said. And it was. I had no desire to approach the bloody scene above. Hell, I didn't even want to be here.

We didn't wait long. When the sheep and goats were gone, having all been bled and tossed to the wicked whirlwinds below, the shepherds did not linger. Nor did they come far down that slope before spotting us. They were unarmed save for the staves and the knife and, though I did not understand their language, I could hear in their tones the anger and fear our guns and uniforms raised in them. They spoke briefly to one another, then one of the younger men directed his voice to us. The old man took the speaker by the arm and moved past him, saying something as he moved toward me and Powell.

"What are they saying?" I asked Powell, for he spoke many of the local dialects.

"The young guy said we don't belong here, but the old man told him to shut up. Looks like he wants to talk."

As the old man walked steadily toward us, Powell called out to him. They exchanged words and I kept my gun raised.

"You going to fill me in?"

"I told him we're soldiers, and we're lost."

"Did you ask him about those things?"

"I'm getting to it," he said. "Lower your weapon."

"Are you shitting me?"

"He's promised peace."

"You're buying that?"

"Put your gun down, Duffy."

I complied and Powell went on speaking to the old

shepherd. A minute later, the old man was signaling the others to approach. We stood there, the six of us, staring at one another beneath the clear sky and blistering sun. Looking at them, at Powell, I couldn't have said which of us had more dried blood caked on our clothes.

"He wants us to take shelter with them," Powell said. "There's a shallow cave nearby with a spring. They use it often."

"How often?" I asked. "Do they perform this sacrifice often?"

"He hasn't said." Powell looked at me. "I haven't asked."

We followed them up the mountain and into a small cave that was damp and cool and very welcome after days wandering the desert. I couldn't recall the last time I'd drunk water. It's possible I was on the verge of death; likely I'd hallucinated much of what I'd believed I'd seen the past twelve hours or so. But Powell had seen it too, and the men with us most certainly had killed all those animals. *Sacrificed* them.

In the back of the shallow cave was a small still pool. The men drew water from it and offered it to me. I hesitated, earning a look of wary consternation from Powell. I wasn't sure if he thought me wise or foolish, but he didn't drink either. One of the younger men looked me in the eye, drank deep, then pressed the wooden cup into my hand.

I took the cup then, and drank gladly, drank greedily. My mouth was dry and cracked and the cool water washed over my insides like a healing balm applied to a burn, soothing me, quenching me. Physically, it was what I'd needed; psychologically, I was still in need of assuagement. What had I seen out there in the desert? What were those things? How were these men so calm in the face of something so monstrous? I wanted nothing more than to return to base, to be in a world that made sense to me; but I was here now and wanted to understand, if it was in my grasp to comprehend.

"Ask them," I said.

Powell nodded and guzzled another cup of water. He spoke to the old man, and I sat silently while the old man responded.

"They call them The Thirsty," Powell said. "Demons, or fallen angels, who long ago shed the blood of men. They came from beyond, and when they came to Earth, they began to prey on the beasts of the land, not differentiating between man and any other creature. This angered...I think he means God, or a god." Powell shook his head, as if he'd lost the trail of the old man's words.

The two of them spoke among themselves briefly. Feeling the weight of eyes upon me, I turned to the other men in the cave. They were staring at me, watching me. It occurred to me that I could very well be their next sacrifice. I tried to no avail to push that thought from my mind.

"The Thirsty were cursed," Powell said. "Punished. They must feed upon blood, but they are forbidden to shed blood. Their physical forms were—destroyed? banished? stripped? —but their essence is confined always to the sand."

"So, they need blood spilled for them?" I asked.

"What do you mean?"

"What would these things do if these men simply stopped giving them blood?"

Powell relayed my question. The old man spoke. Powell looked at me. "He says The Thirsty can whisper to men in their dreams or invade their minds."

"Possess them?" I asked.

"No," Powell said, shaking his head. "Whispers." Powell paused, listening as the old man continued, then his eyes went wide, and his mouth gaped. He turned slowly toward me. "Their minds can reach far, he says. They speak to men and sometimes those men believe they are hearing the voice of a god or an angel. The Thirsty tell these men to go to war, to conquer, to kill."

"They cause war?" I asked. It was just crazy enough to make sense. Well, as much sense as I'd ever made of any war.

"They need it," Powell said. "These men." He motioned to those in the cave. "Their village has not been involved in a war in more than a thousand years. No other people come to this area; they don't make it this far. The Thirsty are content to drink the blood of lambs and goats, and as long as the village provides blood, they are left in peace."

"But everyone else has to fight?"

"They have to bleed," Powell said. "These things—The Thirsty—are the reason for the conflict in this part of the world."

"Going back how far?"

"He says, forever."

"How do we stop them?" I asked. "Can we kill them, put an end to war?"

Powell spoke again to the old man. I took another cup of water and drank it. The young men in the cave were eerily silent and seemed content to sit watching me. I looked into each of their eyes there in the dimness of the cave, searching for something in their expressions. There was nothing revealing in their eyes or on their faces, only the merest curiosity and perhaps a sense of invasion. I was an outsider here. I did not belong.

It occurred to me then that the events of this day were not strange for these people. This was simply a part of their life. Did they know that the rest of the world was unaware of the Thirsty? Did they realize that the rest of us went on fighting wars to feed these ancient entities without knowing what we were doing? Without understanding what we were even fighting for?

The old man stopped speaking and Powell turned to me once more. "They cannot be stopped," he said. "They can't be killed. The Thirsty were confined to the sand, and they will stay in the sand until there is no more sand."

"So, we will always have war?"

Powell smiled weakly. "I think even Jesus told us we'd always have war."

~

The Thirsty

After drinking our fill, we left the cave. In the distance, I could hear the sound of sonic booms from fighter planes and the soft thump of far-off explosions. The shepherds moved off, heading up into the mountains on a well-traveled rocky path.

Powell and I set off across the desert, moving toward the sounds of war. This time we had full canteens of water and some sense of the direction we should walk if we were to reach civilization.

"They drink fresh blood," Powell said as we hiked across the low foothills of the small range. "That's what the old man said. They can't harm us, The Thirsty. They drink the blood of the fallen, of the wounded and bleeding."

"So, the dried blood isn't an issue?"

"Nope." Powell shook his head and set his eyes on the horizon. "The old man assured me, Duffy. We'll be fine. We just have to keep moving toward the sound of battle."

How strange it was for me to walk across that sand knowing what lay beneath, knowing that the things there caused this war, wanted it, and that they desired the very blood that was coursing through me, keeping me alive. When they began to thirst, would they begin to speak to me, to interrupt (or intercept) my prayers and push me to shed blood on their behalf? Would they prod me to kill Powell, or to kill myself? What were they capable of? I was left with so many questions as I walked on, following Powell.

He was equally silent, lost in his own contemplations. Perhaps he was thinking the very things I was. Maybe he was listening for them, listening *to* them. It is possible that all the things I was afraid of in that moment were happening to Powell and he was being prompted to kill me. I could have asked him, if only I'd thought of it a moment sooner. But as it happened, it didn't matter much what either of us thought about the war, the desert, The Thirsty. All our thoughts were overshadowed in the sandy, windblown moment by the soft click in the sand and Powell's sudden stillness.

He stood motionless and heaved a deep, audible sigh. "Well," he said. "Shit."

"Stay still," I told him. "I can try to disarm it." I went to a knee and began sweeping sand away from the mine.

"No," he said. "No sense in us both dying out here."

"You don't have to die."

"Have to sometime, Duffy."

I looked up at him and followed his gaze as he peered across the vast empty land toward the sounds of combat.

"If I have to choose between bullets, bombs and boogeymen," he said, "I guess I'll take the bomb beneath my foot." He motioned his head toward my destination. "We were heading there, weren't we?"

"Yes," I said.

"Maybe you'd do better to skirt that area." He shrugged and I winced, waiting for the explosion. "Go find yourself somewhere peaceful to lay low, avoid combat, avoid bloodshed."

"Maybe I will. If you let me try to disarm this mine, the

two of us can find that place together."

He shook his head. "No, Duffy. I'm the demolitions guy. You're a medic. I don't see a way out of this. Besides, I suppose I'm ready." Powell cast his gaze out over the desert, the sand hazy with the heat of the day. He was searching for them, wondering if The Thirsty were lingering nearby. He looked back at me, his eyes meeting mine. "You go on now," he continued. "Just walk on toward the horizon; you'll run into someone eventually. I'll stand as long as I can, make sure you're well out of range."

"I can't leave you here, Powell."

"Yes, you can. Go on now." He hesitated a moment and watched me as I watched him. For a while, neither of us knew what to say. Then he continued, "Look, kid, I've lived a full life. I've fought a lot of battles and seen a lot of things. Bullets and bombs I can deal with. Insurgents, terrorists, combatants. But this…" he motioned around us to the vast expanse of sand, at The Thirsty laying beneath the surface of the desert. "This might be more than I can deal with."

"You don't have to do this."

"We're soldiers, Duffy. In the end, that always mean dying so someone can live."

"So, that's it?"

He nodded. "That's it."

I stood there with him, looking into his eyes, not wanting to leave. Not wanting to face the desert alone. Not wanting to bring this story back without him to corroborate it. But he was resigned. It was there, gleaming in his eyes: Powell couldn't live in a world where such creatures were real. He'd gotten to choose, and he'd taken the bomb over the boogeymen.

Good for him, I guess.

He gave me his canteen and I left him standing there in the sun. It didn't occur to me that I could have taken two steps and hit another mine, but somehow, I pushed on through the dunes, pressing toward the horizon, and never happened upon one.

I must have been half a mile away when Powell lifted his foot. The explosion seemed close, the blast carrying across the flat land to my ears as if I were standing next to him. Startled, I whirled around and saw only a small smattering of scarlet mist in the puff of smoke and the seismic stirring of sentient sand.

~~~

Notes on The Thirsty

The Thirsty *was written with a specific market in mind, though I don't recall the press or the publication name. Ultimately, it was not what they were looking for. My writing groups, however, showed this story much love and many of them agreed (to my dismay) that this may be the best story in this collection.*

The market call I answered with this tale called for stories in which a creature needed blood to sustain itself, with a very specific caveat. No vampires. So, nixing the vampires, I created something a bit new, but perhaps a bit recognizable too.

Blood and Shadow

The most intense conflicts, if overcome, leave behind a sense of security and calm that is not easily overcome.

—Carl Jung

Blood and Shadow

It was two o'clock in the morning on a Saturday when I glimpsed the first one.

I should have known that something was wrong the moment I woke up. I never get up in the middle of the night. Never. But on this night, I awoke from a dream that I couldn't recall, but which had frightened me. I woke in a cold sweat, stifling a scream. When I looked at Sabrina, she had that look of divine beauty that is only really attainable in the midst of deep, peaceful sleep. I hadn't disturbed her.

Still, I was terrified.

I crept out of bed and went to check on the children. The girls shared a room, and I stopped there first. I stepped into the dark of their bedroom and into the light of the full moon beaming through the window. The window was open, the cool night's breeze billowing the drapes and bringing with it leaves of gold and red and green and orange. The night was clear and calm. The sky was filled with stars. Autumn in Michigan is beautiful, unless it's two a.m. and you're scared out of your wits, and you're not sure why.

Kate—who was now sixteen and most certainly no

longer Katie!—was curled up like a baby, sleeping with her back to the room, face to the wall, arms wrapped around her childhood teddy. Her arms tightened and relaxed around the bear's neck as she dreamed.

Across the room Anna, our youngest, lay on her back, long dark hair draped over the edge of the bed, limbs akimbo, the way six-year-olds seem to be programmed to lay while sleeping, wore that same angelic mask that her mother was wearing in our bedroom down the hall. I was tempted to readjust her and cover her, but to what end? She seemed comfortable enough. Anna's chest rose and fell rhythmically; she was breathing and dreaming. She was fine.

So why was my heart still flailing? I could hear it pulsing in my ears. I was still sweating, and the dampness of my shirt was making me cold.

Slipping out, closing the door behind me, I moved down the hall, passing the bathroom, and stopped outside Glen's room. His light was on. What on earth was he doing awake at two in the morning? I could think of a few things I'd have been doing in the middle of the night at thirteen, so I resisted the urge to turn the handle and barge in. I knocked softly and waited. Twenty seconds passed and there was no answer. I knocked again, louder this time. There were voices inside; Glen was talking to someone. I couldn't make out what he was saying. Still, he didn't answer. The door was locked. Glen's voice was raised. He sounded angry. He swore, which was out of character for him. But he was thirteen and I was his dad, what did I know? He probably swore around his friends all the time. But who was he talking to in the middle of the night? Had he smuggled his girlfriend in? Did he have a girlfriend this week? Was someone staying over, and had I forgotten about it? If so, why did he sound so angry? What the hell was going on in there?

The urge came to me to shoulder my way through the door. Instead, I went back to my bedroom, careful not to wake Sabrina, and retrieved my cell phone from the nightstand. Standing in the bathroom, I called Glen's phone. To my surprise, he answered on the second ring.

"Dad?"

"Is everything okay?" I said.

"Yeah. I'm fine. Why are you calling me in the middle of the night?"

"I heard you talking to someone. You have company?"

"I'm playing Elder Scrolls Online. Didn't mean to wake you, sorry."

"You didn't wake me. Keep it down though, huh? We don't want to wake your sisters."

"Okay. Sorry."

"No problem. And unlock your door, will you? If I knock and don't get an answer, I'd like to be able to look in on you."

"Fine. Whatever."

He hung up and I went down to the kitchen. I was awake now, and jittery. What was wrong with me? Nothing I could pinpoint, but I figured checking the wards wouldn't hurt.

Blood and Shadow

When we moved into this house ten years earlier, I'd taken care to place protective wards in the yard, surrounding the house, defending my family against any foulness, any of the dark things that were once part of my life. I'd walked away from that world long ago, shortly after meeting Sabrina, but my leaving it behind didn't stop that world from existing all around us. Didn't stop the dark things from roaming the night, from sensing me and my power and seeking me out from time to time. Knowing that dark creatures and dark magic abound in the world is both a boon and a bane. Having the power to defend those you love against those who could (and would, given the opportunity) harm them was a blessing, even if the source of that power was a curse.

I felt it the moment I entered the kitchen. The unmistakable tingle in my spine that signaled their presence. Meropa's Hounds. How many? I didn't know. But they travel in packs. Why hadn't I sensed them earlier? I glanced out the window above the sink. A flat-faced shadow with two dark, narrow slits for nostrils peered in at me. This one had taken the shape of a man, for now.

The Hounds are trackers born of shadow. They morph into whatever shape the situation calls for. Had I not been attuned to them, I would not have seen this one standing there in the dark, with only the full moon to illuminate its silhouette.

Meropa had found me. How? And why now? That old feud had died with his brother during the reign of

Friemund, the faerie king. Afterward, I gave up the use of blood magic. I'd married Sabrina and moved on, telling myself I would never again invoke the curse; but now the shadowmancer had tracked me down, using his insidious Hounds, I knew I'd be forced to call upon my power—my curse—if I was to protect my family.

The thing at the window pressed itself against the glass, its black ethereal body sliding like liquid over the smooth surface, seeking a shadow it could meld into. The light wouldn't keep it out forever. Once it found a shadow to slip into, it would step through, using the darkness as a gate.

Upstairs, Kate screamed.

I grabbed a package of thawed burger from the refrigerator and ran for the stairs. Frozen meat wouldn't do. Bounding up the stairs, I ripped a hole in the plastic, tipped the package, and poured the cold blood into my mouth. I swallowed. It slid down my throat and splashed into my stomach like an early April rainstorm.

Power surged through me, firing inside my body like explosive charges or pistons in an engine. For more than fifteen years I had avoided blood at every turn, never licking a wound, never kissing a child's boo-boo, always cooking my steaks to well-done. This first taste of raw blood after so many years was a fire in my gut. Strength ran through my arms and legs as I bounded down the hall and threw open the door to my daughters' bedroom.

Sabrina was in the hall, her bathrobe wrapped around her, but not fastened.

"What is it?" she said.

"Stay back," I told her.

"Dear Lord," Sabrina said. "Is that blood?"

I wiped my hand across my mouth. When I pulled it away, there was cold cow's blood smeared on my hand. I felt the chill as it dripped from my chin.

I dropped the hamburger in the hall and stepped into the girls' room.

Kate was on her feet in the dark—brave girl that she was—kicking at small dark animals scurrying around the bedroom floor and beating her fists against something larger looming over her sister's bed. A Hound had taken the form of a hideous bat-thing and was standing over Anna, its murky wings spread against the moonbeams in the window, its long, slender fingers probing into my little girl's head. Anna squirmed and groaned, caught in the trap of a Hound-induced nightmare.

Summoning strength that I had not felt in many years, I focused my will into the overhead light, closing the circuit. The light flashed on. The dozen Hounds on the floor had taken the shapes of small critters the size of squirrels and seemed bent on keeping Kate from coming to Anna's aid. It was just like Meropa to torture a little girl, to drive her insane through nightmares. He had always been a coward, preying on the weak, avoiding open confrontation. All these years he had been biding his time, stewing in his hatred. At last, it seemed he was ready to attack me, but he hadn't come for me at all. He had come for my children. Meropa was going to avenge his brother by driving my children mad through terror, the way he and Servetus had tortured those tourists in South Haven. I'd had to confront Servetus. How could Meropa blame me for intervening? I'd had to defend those girls. But Meropa would never forgive me for what happened. I suppose, if he'd killed my brother, maybe I could never forgive him either.

The dim light in the room was not enough to force the Hounds to flee. It would need to be much more intense.

"Dad," Kate yelled. "What are they? What's happening?"

"Get to Glen's room, Kate," I said. "Run. Now."

Kate was on her bed now, knees drawn to her chest. She was staring wide-eyed at the things in the room. All bravado had fled from her. Now she was just a scared girl.

"Brad!" Sabrina screamed. "What's wrong with Anna?"

She blew by me like a fierce wind, racing toward the Hound that was assailing Anna's dreams. But what could she do? What chance did my wife stand against these beasts? Sabrina wasn't born of magic, nor was she cursed as I am, but she had the strength of a mother frightened for her children, ready to fight for them without thought of herself. Not a force to take lightly. As she stepped through the scurrying pack of Hounds, and moved to Anna's side, I realized Sabrina could not see Meropa's Hounds. Of course she couldn't. They were magic-kind and she was not. All Sabrina saw was Anna trembling, apparently having a seizure.

The Hounds on the floor began to grow, most taking the

forms of large dogs now. A few stood on two legs like men; but they were not men. Not even close.

Stretching out an arm, one intercepted Sabrina, its black hand covering her eyes.

Sabrina fell to the ground, her hands to her face, and she screamed. "Brad, I can't see. I'm blind."

"It's temporary," I said.

"What's happening?"

"I can explain later. Right now, I need to focus."

"Focus on what? I'm blind, Brad. Blind!" My wife broke into sobs there on the floor at my feet, and for her own good, and for the sake of our children, I ignored her, giving all my attention over to the battle at hand.

I didn't have much power left. Cold blood doesn't supply the same juice that fresh, warm blood does. Using what strength remained in my veins, I intensified the light in the bulbs overhead, focusing them into a beam, and directed the beam into the bat-Hound that was assaulting Anna. The shaft of light burrowed into the insubstantial shadow and the thing yelped. Its shadow claws retracted from my daughter's mind and the thing leapt out the window, gliding into the moonlight.

The other Hounds were growing, looming large in the little room, threatening to block out what meager light the small overhead bulbs produced. Threatening to darken the room. In full darkness, the agents of the shadowmancer would have the greatest potential and would be at utmost strength.

I had to get my family out of there.

I needed more blood.

Sabrina, blind and terrified, groped in her darkness, screaming, crying. "What's happening, Brad? What's wrong with Anna?"

"Anna's okay," I said. "Kate, take your mom's hand and get her to Glen's room. Now. Move."

My attention was on the growing Hounds. Soon they would eclipse all the light.

Sabrina fought her, but Kate managed to drag her mother into the hall.

I picked Anna up and followed them. Anna was waking now, and as she woke, she screamed. That high, shrill shriek of my horrified little girl. For a moment I was angry. It's funny how that secondary emotion slips through when one is afraid. In the midst of terror, anger creeps in.

Kate screamed again.

In Glen's room, I slammed the door behind me. We were all here, together. Glen pulled off his headphones and turned from his computer. The heavily distorted screams of poorly tuned guitars, accompanied by aggressive drumming and low, loud, growling poured from those headphones. Glen loved his death metal far more than he valued his hearing. It was no wonder he was oblivious to the war just beyond his walls.

"Why are you in my room? What's going on?"

Kate did not answer him. She was staring into the shadows of Glen's closet, where the monster had lived

33

when he was very young. Sabrina had never believed him or the girls when they came with tales of monsters in the night, but I always checked the closets, under beds, the basement, the garage, and the woods beyond the fence. In the beginning, I had been vigilant. The wards had always been in place. When the kids were small, and I was still a newlywed, the threat of my old life had loomed over me. But as the years had passed, and there were no signs of magic-kind, not a hint of sorcery in the air or in my life, I'd become complacent, thinking that Meropa had moved on and forgotten me. I had not checked the wards or reapplied them in a long time. The Hounds had slipped through without as much as a ringing in my ears. Glen's computer monitor gave off its own radiance and someone had switched on the overhead light, but the closet was dark, and in that blackness a mass of insubstantial darkness pulsed in time with the music still blaring from Glen's discard headphones. It was without form, a void, yet there was substance to it, a weight in the darkness, and a presence that Kate felt as much as I did.

"What is it?" Kate asked. "And what were those things in my room?"

"What things?" Sabrina asked. "What's going on? Why can't I see?"

"Didn't you see the things in my room?"

"She can't see them," I said, stepping between my family and the darkness. "She never could."

"Someone tell me what's happening," Sabrina cried.

I said, "I'll explain everything in time. Right now, I need you to stay calm. I'll deal with this."

"How can I stay calm?" Sabrina said. Her voice trailed away, and her eyes fluttered sleepily as I placed my hand on her head, allowing my magic to flow into her as I eased her down onto the bed. Within seconds she was sleeping.

"Deal with what?" Glen asked.

"What did you do?" Kate said.

"I put her to sleep," I said. "She's all right."

"What the hell?" Glen said. His eyes had settled on his closet. Now he saw the thing too, waiting there in the shadows; waiting for the lights in this room to go out. "What is that?"

"The things in your room are Hounds," I told Kate. "That's what we called them. They are servants of an evil man, an old enemy of mine. This is something different. A Mazar. Once the lights go out, the Mazar will leave the closet and—" I didn't know how to say, "it will kill us all," so I said nothing more.

"What enemy," Kate asked. "Since when do you have enemies?"

"Someone you never met. No time for that now. Glen, do you have a knife in here?"

"Just my Swiss army knife," he said. "Not much help in a fight."

"Why couldn't mom see them?" Kate asked.

"She's not magic-kind."

"And we are?" Glen said.

"I am," I said. "And my blood flows in you. You can see them because I can see them."

"What do you mean magic-kind?" Kate asked.

"You'll know soon enough," I told her. "Do you trust me, Glen?"

"Always."

"I need your blood."

"Are you fucking serious?"

"Watch your mouth."

"How much blood?"

"More than you'll want to part with. Cut your arm."

He hesitated. The blade on the Swiss Army knife was open in his hand. He held me with his eyes, weighing his trust in me. He had no idea what I was thinking, what I had in mind and, though I believe he did trust me, I knew what I was asking sounded insane.

The Hounds were working on cutting the electricity. I wondered what had taken them so long, I'd expected this some time ago. I had to do something and do it fast. It wasn't even three o'clock yet; sunrise was still four hours away. The Hounds could move about in light, even sunlight, though they were uncomfortable and limited; but being composed of shadows, the more darkness they had to work in, the stronger they became. Glen's eyes softened and I thought he was going to do as I'd asked, but something unexpected happened. The lights in the room flickered, the screen to his computer monitor flashed, and the computer went into reboot.

Glen had waited too long. In a flurry of panic Kate snatched the knife from her brother and cut a long gouge on the back of her forearm. She grimaced as the blade bit into her flesh. Kate's arm quivered weirdly as tissues separated and blood welled on her soft skin.

"Now what?" she said.

"I need to drink it."

"Go ahead then," she said, holding up her wounded arm, trusting me completely. What a trooper she was then.

"Are you for real right now?" Glen said. "This is sick."

Putting my lips to Kate's arm, I sucked on the warm blood pouring from the cut. The power of fresh blood coursed through me like it had that first time twenty-five years earlier when I'd been working at Bluegrass Meat Processing. I held my daughter's arm in my hands like a rack of ribs, face buried, and mouth opened, drinking in her lifeblood. Her flesh shuddered beneath my lips; there was energy surging through her too. I finished drinking. Her blood dripping from my chin, I looked into her eyes and saw it there: power. Kate possessed a magic similar to mine and her magic had come to her in that moment.

"What is this?" she said.

"I don't know," I told her.

"Something has changed inside me, dad," Kate said. "Something's different."

"I felt it. Now stand back."

"You guys are crazy," Glen said.

"Do you have something that can be crushed to

powder?"

"What?" Glen said.

The Mazar in the closet stirred like a caged beast waiting to be released. It was waiting for the darkness to come.

"I need powder. Anything will do."

"Here," he said, handing me the jar of colored sand from his desk.

"Perfect," I said. I unscrewed the cap and the jar slipped from my hand.

All at once Glen, Kate, and I reached for the tumbling jar as the sand spilled out onto the carpet next to Kate's drying blood. The jar stopped spinning in mid-air, never striking the ground. Kate pulled it to her hand.

"How'd you do that?" Glen asked.

Kate did not respond.

The lights flickered again. The Mazar inched out of the closet, then retreated.

Outside the moon was still high in the sky. Crickets chirped in the field behind the house. In the woods, owls called to each other.

"Kate," I said, "pour the rest of that in my hands."

She poured it out and I held the sand in my cupped hands, infusing it with magic that would cause each grain to light up bright as a star once it clung to its target. It took only moments to enact the magic, but it took everything I had. The magic was taxing. Suddenly, I was tired and weak. I went to one knee. Turning toward the Mazar in the closet, I intended to toss the sand onto the creature and swallow up its folds of shadow in light, but I had no strength left.

"Here, Dad," Kate said, placing the jar under my hands. "Put it back in here." She pried my fingers apart and the sand ran between them, falling back into the jar.

"Cover the Mazar," I said, "Then close your eyes."

"I'll do it," Glen said. "You stay back."

Kate didn't argue. She handed the jar to her brother.

Glen crept toward the closet; the jar of magic sand held out before him. He was shaking. The murky thing in the inky darkness throbbed and pulsated in anticipation. I could feel the shadow monster's yearning. It would feed on the child's fear, then feast on his flesh. I'd dealt with these things before. It had been a Mazar that had finally made me realize what Servetus and Meropa had really been up to two decades ago. I hadn't fully understood the brutality of shadow magic until I had witnessed a summoned Mazar torturing and consuming a girl the brothers had picked up at the beach. I couldn't allow that to happen to my children, but all my strength was spent. It was up to Glen now to get us through the night.

The lights went out.

The Mazar lunged.

There was a flare as the room exploded into sheer white light. My eyes closed instinctively against the brightness. When I opened them all that remained was the light, so bright it was blinding.

"Are you okay?" I asked.

"I can't see," Kate said.

"Glen?"

"I'm all right. The Mazar's gone. I got some of the sand on me. I can't brush it off."

"That's okay," I said. "Leave it. Is all this light coming from you?"

"Yes. I think so. And that pile in the closet."

"This light will last until morning. We'll be safe here."

"Then what?" Kate asked.

"Then I have to go see an old friend. And you two will have to go into the forest."

~

"What's in the drum?" Glen asked me when I pulled into the drive with a 55-gallon barrel in the back of my truck the following afternoon.

I'd driven into Bluegrass to visit my old boss, Hank, at Bluegrass Meat Processing while I'd sent Kate and Glen into the forest with Anna to find Friemund. When I was eighteen and had first discovered my magic, Friemund had found me in that forest. He had been my friend and mentor since. If anyone could explain the nature of magic to my children, it was him. He also had a way of testing one's blood for magical properties. Kate's power had been apparent the night before; I thought having the other two tested would be a good idea. Sending them into the forest was the best thing for them that day. Those woods were protected by faerie magic. Meropa had no power there, even in the shade of the trees.

As I'd suspected, Sabrina's sight had returned in the

morning. Her blindness had been an illusion conjured by a Hound. A scare tactic. The cowards feed on fear. She'd awakened in fright, still demanding answers. I'd taken her with me into Bluegrass, explaining all I could of the truth as I drove. She listened in silence. I don't know how much she believed at the time.

I met Sabrina in college when I was twenty-four. Six years earlier, when I was eighteen and working at Bluegrass Meat Processing, I'd discovered my magic. The guys I worked with told me that I had to eat the heart and drink the blood of my first kill. Of course, they were joshing me, but the idea interested me. I'd heard that many cultures had such a ritual, a passage into manhood, and that a boy was expected to drink the blood of his first kill; in some cultures, it was said that one would drink the blood of the first kill of each season, or of each hunt. Those guys I worked with were not going to let me drink blood. It was a big joke. But something inside me nagged at me. I had to try it. I wanted to drink blood. One day, during lunch, I went to the kill floor and dipped a Styrofoam coffee cup into the barrel that the cow blood drained into and took a drink. The blood was thick and warm, like hot cocoa, and tasted heavily of iron, but it felt right. The moment it hit my stomach, I felt the warmth of energy, and renewed vitality, flowing through me. It was intoxicating. I drank three full cups. Afterward, things began happening to me. I could see glimpses of the future and the past. I could make things move without touching them. I made a pig's heart stop by telling it to stop beating. It was frightening, yet intriguing.

Soon after, I was walking in the woods, these very woods standing behind the house in which I now live with my family, and the faerie, Friemund, sensing the magic in me, came to me.

I told Sabrina this tale as we drove into Bluegrass. She didn't say a word. She said nothing when Hank and I loaded the barrel of blood into my truck. On the way home she said only one thing.

"Are the children safe?" she said.

"Right now," I told her, "they are in the safest place in all the world."

When we arrived home, the children were coming across the yard. They had finished their business in the woods.

Glen was looking at the barrel. "What is it?" he asked.

"Blood," Sabrina said, her voice even and mellow. She was starting to believe, but she didn't want to.

"That's a lot," Anna said.

I hopped out of the truck and tousled her hair.

"It's going to keep us safe," I said. "Did you find him?"

"He found us," Kate said.

"What did you learn?"

Kate and Glen looked at each other.

"A lot," Glen said. "Friemund told us how to use our magic."

"But warned us," Kate said, "To use it seldom."

"What about Meropa?"

"He told us that too," Glen said.

"He told us," Anna said, "That you and Meropa and Servetus used to be friends, but then some bad stuff happened and now you're not friends anymore."

"Sounds about right," I said.

"He told us where to find Meropa," Kate said.

"And that we can stop him," Glen said.

"Kill him," Kate corrected. "He said we would kill him."

"But that one of us would die," Glen said.

"Die?" Sabrina gasped. He wide eyes darted wildly from one child the to next, at last meeting mine.

"Mm-hmm," Anna said.

"One of you kids? Or one of us, the family?" Sabrina asked. There was no doubt that if the choice was hers, Sabrina would die that we all may live. That was her nature, to nurture and protect.

"He didn't say that," Kate said.

"He said, 'one of you'," Glen said.

"We can't kill a man," Sabrina said. "You two should hear yourselves."

"He's not a man," I said.

"He's in Bluegrass," Glen began.

"Staying at the Summer Inn," Kate said, finishing Glen's sentence.

"Still," said Sabrina. "Are you really going to murder someone, Brad?"

"He did," Anna said, indicating me. "A long time ago daddy killed Meropa's brother. The faerie said so."

Sabrina stared at me as if I were a monster. "Is it true?

Blood and Shadow

You murdered someone?"

"Not all killing is murder, sweetheart."

"Why so much blood?" Glen asked.

"Using magic takes a lot out of me. I have to keep fueled. And, depending on what Friemund said, I got enough for you, too."

"Our magic doesn't work that way," Kate said. "We use our own blood."

"We can't go marching into Bluegrass with a barrel of blood and start cutting ourselves and throwing around blood magic in the streets," I said. "Taking the fight to Meropa isn't an option. He's holed up like a coward for a reason. But if his Hounds can't harm me through you guys, capture me, or kill me—which is his ultimate goal—he'll come himself. He's a coward, but he's also determined."

~

He came at twilight of the third day with the shadows stretched long behind him. He was tall and slender, donning a long black coat that made him appear as one with the darkness. Fitting for one so malicious and cruel. Meropa brought with him a legion of shadow Hounds and a dozen Mazar. He thought he had only me to contend with.

I had enlisted Glen's and Kate's help in reworking the wards to flash into bright lights when they were tripped. Glen's particular skill set allowed for a variation that would be useful. He was a master of elements, according to Friemund; earth, wind, and fire were his allies. That would weaken the Hounds and Mazar, but Meropa would have other methods of attack. He was not a servant of the shadows, but their master; he would bend the darkness to his will and use it against me and my family. I'd used as much of the blood from the drum as I could while it was still fresh, placing wards and enchanting the grounds. Now my supply of fresh, warm blood was running low. Kate and I had placed extra protection around the living room to protect Sabrina (who could not see the Hounds or Mazar) and Anna (who I didn't want in the midst of the battle).

The first wave of Hounds came in various forms and sizes. When they crossed the boundary of my property, the first of the wards exploded into fire, encircling the house in light and heat. Many Hounds retreated. All of the Mazar vanished. They would return, I knew, but there were other wards in place.

I stood with Kate and Glen in the drive as Meropa approached. He didn't hesitate. He'd spent too many years hunting me to waste time on conversation. He hurled darkness at us, eclipsing the light from the fire, and giving his minions a bridge to cross the gap to us. In rushed Hounds, leaping like great cats, charging like bulls, snarling like wolves. The battle began.

Glen and Kate each wielded a knife. Each cut into their own flesh, conjuring power from their veins. The use of their magic was instinctual, as if they had been using these gifts all their lives.

Glen pushed the line of fire back over the shadow bridge conjured by the shadowmancer, cutting off the rushing wave of Hounds from the host of Meropa's legion. Hounds scattered, searching for shadows. Their power was darkness. Their life was obscurity and gloom. Light, for them, was fear and death.

I spun a globe of shimmering light around a group of charging Hounds, trapping them inside and shrinking the sphere into nothingness, obliterating the monsters.

Kate lifted the hem of her shirt and cut a small swath of flesh from her side, screaming in agony, sacrificing pain and health for a large amount of power. Like our adversary, she was wasting no time. The determination in her eyes told me that she would give herself to save the rest of us. She would not tiptoe around it. It would be Kate, I thought. She would be the one to die tonight. Her hands covered in her own blood, Kate reached to the heavens. The clouds parted. In the sky the stars and moon were barely visible. Night had not yet come in its fullness.

After two more globes of shimmering light and a banishment that eliminated two Mazar, I was spent and needed blood. All that remained was cold and two days old: coagulated and thick. It would have to do.

I turned to head into the garage.

There, in the light, in the door of the garage, stood Anna, small and frail in the shadow of the night. She had left the protection of the living room. She had come out into the fray. What could such a little girl do against such viscous, wild hate? Meropa was bent on destroying us. He walked forward calmly, only a hundred yards away, sending waves of magic and monsters at us in the guise of shadows. And here stood little Anna, holding only a sewing needle.

"Go back inside, honey," I said.

"I can help," she said.

"Help your mommy."

"I will," Anna said. "But first, I'll help you."

She pricked the tip of her finger with the needle and squeezed drops of blood into the dirt at her feet. Each drop grew into a puddle and from each puddle climbed small, monkey-like creatures made of congealed blood. Anna had called to the blood in the barrel, and somehow, she had breathed false life into it. There were dozens of the monkey-things. The creatures rushed forward in a frantic wave, weaving around me, then around Kate and Glen, flinging themselves into fierce mêlée with the Hounds.

Meropa came on undaunted, his conjured forces falling all around him. As Meropa reached the edge of the yard, Glen cut a line across his leg, allowing the blood to flow down to the earth. He stomped his foot three times and the earth rose and fell before him like a wave tossed in the ocean. Meropa was thrown off balance and stumbled. He fell to his knees. Shadow enveloped him. He vanished, then stepped out of shadow ten yards from Glen wielding a concentrated beam of shadow as if it were a dark sword.

Meropa plunged the shadow blade into Glen's belly.

"No!" Kate screamed, and I echoed her.

Glen spat blood in Meropa's face. The blood congealed into a hard shell over the shadowmancer's mouth and nose, suffocating him. Meropa reeled about, scratching at the hardened mask, unable to breathe. Glen held tight to Meropa, not giving the shadowmancer any respite. Meropa's magic was no use to him without air in his lungs. The blood flowing from Glen's belly cocooned around them. A hole opened in the earth beneath them as the red cocoon formed around them, lines of blood stringing itself like yarn until I could no longer see my son or my enemy. The pod lay in the ground like a gruesome seed.

Without a master the Hounds and Mazar vanished, whether dissolving into the night, or simply retreating into darkness, I don't know. Anna's blood monkeys fell into oozing puddles and seeped into the ground.

It was over. Meropa was dead. And, as Friemund had warned the children, one of them had died. I think Glen knew all along it would be him, though I'd thought that it would be Kate. Kate had had that look in her eye; that look of determination and sacrifice. Maybe she'd intended to be the one, to bleed herself dry to protect the family. Maybe she was trying to fulfil the faerie's prophecy before it claimed someone else.

I led the girls inside to their mother, who had been watching from the window and was weeping when we came inside.

There would be no monsters tonight. Not under beds, or in closets, or in the garage, or in the basement. There was one buried in the yard, cocooned in a tomb with the bravest boy I ever knew, but he would not be bothering us anymore.

I drank what blood I had left and used what magic I could to heal Kate's wounds. I couldn't do much for her, though she survived.

Her body is scarred. It always will be until she can find a way to regenerate. She speaks of it often, her search for healing magic, but I don't think she's come to it yet.

Anna refuses to use her magic these days. Summoning monsters, she says, to fight other monsters, seems wrong.

Sabrina planted a weeping willow over the spot where Glen lies. She spends most of her time out there. I spend most of my time with her, under the tree.

~ ~ ~

Notes on Blood and Shadow

Blood and Shadow *is the oldest story in this collection, written maybe ten years before most of the others. I don't recall what I was thinking, or what I was reading at the time of this writing. I am an avid Dungeons and Dragons player, and I partake in many other tabletop role-playing games. Given the nature of magic and the relationships between characters in this story, I would guess this tale was inspired by my role-playing group.*

Henry Hatchett

Where are they gone, the old familiar faces?
I had a mother, but she died, and left me,
Died prematurely in a day of horrors—
All, are gone, the old familiar faces.

Charles Lamb
from *The Old Familiar Faces*

Henry Hatchett

His name was Henry Hatchett, and it had been working against him for damn near twenty years.

Henry Hatchett was a butcher by trade, working long days at Main Street Meats, and enjoying the taste of a cold beer down at Dolly's after quitting time. When Henry started working here, he didn't love it, but old Vince Walker was the only man in town willing to give Henry a job. Most folks simply shunned Henry Hatchett in the days and months following the Camp Cado Massacre. Few accepted him now. Even after his exoneration, the majority of folks in Cado Lake, Michigan, still thought of Henry as the Camp Cado Cutter.

Over the years, Henry learned to love the butchering trade, for it was all he had to support himself and his son, Jack.

For the first dozen years of Jack's life, Henry hadn't seen much of him. Nancy had left Henry after the massacre at the cabin and though she never said one way or the other if she believed Henry had killed those people, killed his friends and his own sister, Nancy had not hesitated to call off the engagement and cut all ties with Henry. Who could blame her? The stink of stigma clung to Henry like the scent of death in a slaughterhouse, and by extension it befouled Nancy too.

When Jack turned thirteen, the courts finally agreed that Henry had a legal right to see his son. A year later, at just 32, Nancy died in a car crash. It had been just Henry and Jack since then.

He was in the back room, cutting ribeye steaks with a long, curved knife. Henry preferred the back, away from the counter, away from the customers, far away from the haunting taunts of the cruel nursery rhymes in which he figured prominently. When cutting meat, Henry longed for the old days, dreamt of long weekends of fishing, swimming, camping, hunting, as he and his friends were wont to do, like they had on that hot summer evening nearly two decades past. Reminiscing was better than thinking about the meat and the knife. If he focused too much on the meat, the blood, the blades, his mind would slip back to that night in the cabin on Cado Lake.

As a rule, he thought only of the days before the massacre. But sometimes the memories and images of that night assaulted him, slipping in at the worst moments, triggered by a look from someone, a phrase spoken, a whisper followed by averted eyes.

He could still see their faces, the dead faces of his sister, Vicky, and his other friends. Their cold, sightless eyes would stare at him amid the blood, the carnage, the laughter of the four masked villains who had come upon them in the night. He saw them, too, sometimes, a quartet of killers in gawdy Halloween masks, dressed as monsters. Dressed to kill. He had heard their voices as they slashed and gouged. He'd watched them prance and pounce, giggling all the while, as one-by-one the sinister foursome had slaughtered his friends.

Henry had been tied to a chair, arms bound behind him, legs strapped to the chair legs. They hadn't gagged him. Why would they? Henry and his friends had been the only people on the lake. He hated himself for never leaving this town, never shedding the nightmares and the fear. Mostly, he hated himself for surviving, for living when the others had died.

There was a sound behind him, a voice, calling Henry's name. Henry's hand twitched, tightening on the hilt of the curved knife and he whirled about, knife arm tensed and ready to slash.

Joel Walker, son of Vince, stepped back, his wary eyes searching Henry's face, watching Henry's hands, his eyes narrow, his lips pursed, his round jaw slack. He raised his hands palms out. "Calm down there, boss," Joel said. Joel always called Henry boss, which they both thought was funny since Henry worked for Joel and his brother Ethan since their father had died four years back. "Jack's up front asking for you. You want to come out, or want me to send him back?"

Henry blinked slowly, shrugged, and set the knife down

on the table. Wiping his hands on his once-white apron, he said, "I'll come out."

Beyond the doors, the small building opened into a lobby with freezers and coolers packed with meat. Customers queued at the counter, their eyes falling in unison upon Henry. Joel and two other men were packing up meat in butcher's paper while Ethan worked the register. On the far side of the counter stood Jack, who was the very image of his father when Henry was seventeen, except Jack's hair was red like his mothers, and Henry's was black.

"Hatchett Henry," a young man cried in mock horror, swinging his arm in a chopping motion.

As if on cue, a young girl in line with her mother began chanting, "One, two, Henry lost a screw."

"Susan," the girl's mother chided through clenched teeth, yanking the girl's arm hard enough to bring both tears and wailing.

Henry saw Jack grin when the girl began to cry. "Everything okay?"

"I want to ask you something," Jack said.

"Three, four, found him covered in gore." This was a man's deep baritone, and it was cut off by Ethan, who glared hard at the man and slammed the register shut.

"Out!" Ethan shouted, pointing to the door and not taking his eyes from the customer. "Lifetime ban, Pete."

"Ah, come on," Pete protested. "You can't be serious."

"I'm not playing with you, Pete. You've been warned. Now, get out, and don't come back."

Henry's face was burning. He could feel sweat on his cheeks. "Come on in back, Jack. We'll talk there." He was working to keep the sadness from his voice, but he knew he was failing. After seventeen years, it still hurt to think that people believed he had killed his own sister.

Henry led Jack into the cutting room. "Sorry you had to hear that."

"I don't listen to that shit, Dad. You shouldn't either."

Henry grinned but couldn't bring himself to meet his son's eyes. "I've got two hours till I'm off, Jack."

Jack took a deep breath and looked pointedly away from his father. "Some of the guys are going camping this weekend."

It felt like a vice was crushing Henry's chest. Every muscle tensed. Breathing seemed suddenly difficult. His left eye twitched as he leaned back against the cutting table, one hand squishing a ribeye steak. "No," he said. It was reflexive, instinctive.

"I know," Jack said. "You don't want me to go."

"You can't," Henry said.

"I'll be fine," Jack said.

"You don't know that."

"We just graduated, Dad. The guys want to go out and celebrate."

"Drink, you mean."

"Probably. Yeah. But we want to go out to Felldown Forest and camp, so we won't be on the road. We won't be near anybody."

"That's my concern," Henry said.

"I'm sorry about what happened to you," Jack said. He was staring at his father now.

Henry met Jack's eyes. "You don't know what happened to me."

"Everyone knows what happened to you."

"They seem to think so."

"I've pieced enough together over the years; but I've never heard it from you."

"Maybe you should."

They fell silent then, staring at one another. The humming of the air conditioner was like a storm in Henry's ears. He couldn't believe he'd just said that. He'd never spoken of the killings with anyone other than the police. Henry had never sought counseling, had never explained it to Nancy, not even Joel and Ethan had heard the tale from Henry's lips.

"You mean it?"

Henry looked away, looked up at the clock. Not meeting Jack's eyes, he said, "Tell you what, Jack. If you want to go camping this weekend…" Henry swallowed hard. "Why don't you and I go rent a cabin?"

Jack eyed his father skeptically. "I've begged you to take me camping for years. To take me hunting, fishing. I want to go with my friends."

In truth, Henry was relieved. The last thing he wanted to do was stay in a cabin in the woods. Being alone in his apartment scared him enough. He looked up at the clock on the wall. In two hours, he'd be down to Dolly's with Ethan and Joel and he'd be there for most the night. Hell, maybe all night. Henry felt like he could use a night's worth of drinks now. "I'll think about it."

Jack's shoulders sagged. He stared hard at his father, his neck flushed, his eyes narrowed. "They wanted to leave before dark."

"I'll call you in a few hours," Henry said. "Let me think about it."

"So, you're saying no."

"Just give me a couple hours."

"You never let me do anything," Jack sneered. "It's bad enough you let your fear control *you*; but it shouldn't control me too." He pushed through the doors and headed back into the storefront.

Henry wanted to follow him, to argue, to tell Jack that all Henry wanted, all he'd ever wanted, was to protect those he'd loved. But what good would that do? What good had it ever done?

He saw Vicky's face then, smeared with blood and tears, gaping up at him like a dying fish. He saw the twisted black-and-white clown mask of the slim woman crouched before him, running her knife up and down his thigh, threatening to carve him up, beginning at his belt. "Any last requests?" she'd said. And of course, Henry had had one last request. The one that had made him Hatchett Henry, The Camp Cado Cutter, the request that had ended his life more surely than that crazy quartet would have ended it that night.

Henry Hatchett

"Cut the ropes," he'd said. "Let me go." It was a desperate bid he'd made. Henry could never explain why he'd said it, nor could he explain why the psychotic woman had said, "Sure."

In the sweetest little girl voice Henry had ever heard, she said, "Sure," then she'd cut him loose and sent him on his way, slipping in the blood of his friends, fleeing the massacre, racing into the woods and running till he'd reached the highway.

He should have died that night. Death would have been better than seventeen years of looking over his shoulder, waiting for the killers to come for him. It would have been better than listening to the chiding calls and nursery rhymes, the cruel names and dirty looks. It would have been better than being shunned, ostracized, living as an outcast in his own hometown. And it sure as shit would have been better for Jack that Henry had died that night with the others, a victim, instead of living to be the monster the whole town perceived him to be.

~

Jack had known his father would say no. He always said no. Hell, Jack wasn't allowed to sleep over at a friend's house; why would he be allowed to go camping? It had been that way ever since his mom had died. Sometimes Jack wished he'd never met his father. It was hard being Hatchett Henry's son. To his shame, Jack often wished his father had died in that cabin seventeen years ago. At least then he would never have been a suspect in the murders.

Why did he even bother asking for permission? He knew how his dad would respond. Now Jack was disobeying his father by leaving with the others and hiking into Felldown Forest. There were four of them: Jack and his girlfriend, Mia, along with Noah and his new girlfriend, Riley.

"How'd you convince your dad to let you come?" Noah asked, leading the way through the trees on a path familiar to him.

"He's cool," Jack said. "Sometimes."

"I'm sure glad you're here." Mia squeezed Jack's hand and kissed his cheek.

"Doesn't it scare you?" Riley asked. "Being out here? Camping?"

"Not so much." Jack didn't look back at her, nor did his pace vary. "It's terrible, what happened back then, but it was before I was born. I'm not scared of the woods."

"It was a cabin, though," Noah said.

"Right." Riley's head bobbed in agreement. "I heard that. A cabin at Camp Cado Lake."

Mia tugged at Jack's hand, quickening her pace and pulling him along, moving him away from the others. He appreciated her effort. When Jack was with other people, the conversation seemed to always lead back to his father and the killings. That had all happened seventeen years earlier, while his mother was pregnant. He didn't know the truth of what had happened, only what he'd gathered from rumors, from campfire tales, from old papers and police reports. Before his mother had died, most of Jack's

61

knowledge of his father had come to him in lore, from the legend that overshadowed Cado Lake, the legend of Hatchett Henry.

But now Jack felt he knew his father well, knew the man's fears, moods, beliefs, habits; Jack would wager he knew Henry better than anyone. Though his father made his life difficult, Jack didn't believe for one moment that he was a killer. Jack considered himself a good judge of character. Henry was a decent man who had been a victim of something terrible. He was a little weird, but he tried to be normal. For as much as Jack wanted to hate Henry sometimes, he found himself pitying his father. It wasn't really Henry's fault any of this had happened; wasn't his fault he'd become a local legend.

"When are the others coming?" Jack called back to Noah.

"In a bit. Caleb had to work."

"Don't let them upset you tonight," Mia said softly in Jack's ear. "Caleb is a jerk, and he gets Noah going."

"I know." Jack forced a grin. "I'll be fine."

~

The bar smelled of beer, sweat, and spirits. In the distance, Reba sang *The Night the Lights went out in Georgia* from a jukebox. The sounds of billiard balls crashing together and glasses rattling on trays formed a sort of background medley to accompany the chorus of murmurs and friendly ribbing that filled the room.

Henry was perched on his usual stool at Dolly's, flanked

by Ethan and Joel, the only men he had to call friends. He was three beers in and locked in a solemn staring contest with his reflection. In the beginning, shortly after the killings, Henry had hated coming in here with the Walker brothers. He'd loathed the looks he got from people, the comments they'd make, the blunt way many of the drunks would march up to him and spit insults, calling him a murderer. It had been a long, hard road, but Ethan and Joel had walked it with him, pushing and pulling at Henry every step of the way, working to help him achieve some semblance of a normal life.

After all these years, it just may have worked. From the outside, Henry was just your average guy, working the eight-to-five and hanging out with his friends afterward. Inside, however, Henry was a tangle of nerves, always waiting for the next conflict, ever vigilant for the return of the costumed killers. Few others seemed to believe Henry Hatchett's tale of the carnival-clad coven who had come into the cabin and killed everyone except him. *Why would they just let you go?* It was a question he'd asked himself every day since that night.

They were out there, and Henry knew it. Those killers knew his face, but he didn't know theirs. Though they had let him run away all those years ago, fleeing through the sand and high grass, racing through the woods spattered with the blood of his friends, wiping his sister's blood from his face, Henry had never shaken the feeling that they were nearby, watching him, laughing their evil laughs together at his expense; and he did not doubt they would come for him again. Or worse, the unspoken fear that they would come for Jack and take away the one thing Henry had left.

Had the Camp Cado killers—the *real* killers—known Nancy was pregnant? Had they known that Henry was expecting a child and would spend the rest of his life in terror of them coming to take that child away? Henry had never stopped thinking of them. They were in his dreams, in every face he met on the street, in each voice, lurking in every shadow. He was horrified whenever Jack was out of sight, certain they were coming for the boy. That was why Henry insisted Jack carry the knife.

"You have to let him go sometime," Joel said. "He's seventeen. Remember being seventeen, Henry? Could anybody tell us what to do?"

"Hell no," Ethan said from Henry's other side. "We did whatever we wanted."

Henry didn't answer them. Of course, he remembered being a stupid kid. He knew he couldn't control Jack forever; but what kind of man would he be if he didn't protect his son?

"He'll be eighteen soon, won't he?" Ethan shoved a chili-lathered waffle fry into his mouth and followed it with a shot of whiskey.

"A few months," Henry murmured.

"Nothing you can do then," Joel said. "He'll resent you for holding him back."

"I can't just let him go."

"I'm not going to tell you how to raise your boy, Henry."

"But?"

"But you should let him go," Ethan supplied.

"I get it," Joel said. "You're scared to lose him. More scared than most parents. Hell, I don't blame you."

"Me neither," Ethan said.

"But," Joel continued, "if you hold on too tight, you will lose him. No doubt."

"If he never spoke to me again, at least he'd be safe."

"You can't know that. The world is dangerous for everyone. Anything could happen, Henry."

"That's what scares me."

"Let the kid go camping with his friends," Ethan said. "There's no way the same thing could happen to a father and son all these years apart."

"Zero percent chance," Joel said.

Henry drained his beer and asked for another, then resumed his staring contest with the man in the mirror. Judging by the look in his reflection's eyes, Henry didn't think he was sure that was true. He couldn't look at his friends, he couldn't look at Dolly standing behind the counter as she pushed another beer his way. But he heard her when she said, "They're right, hon. Got to let the boy fly sometime. Can't let *your* ghosts haunt *him* now, can you?"

"Maybe you're right," Henry said. "But some things you don't get over."

"Nobody is saying get over it," Joel said.

"Just don't let it control you," Dolly offered. She was a

bouncing, perky woman; one of those pushing-forty women who had reverted to a high-pitched high-school voice and tried to squeeze into teenage vernacular. She called everybody "hon." Henry didn't mind. It made him feel a bit normal.

Ethan popped another waffle fry into his mouth and smacked loudly. "Don't let it drive your son away."

"Besides," said Dolly, "didn't you say he's camping in the woods? It's a different scenario. Not like it's the same cabin."

The three men stared at her, mouth gaping, eyes wide.

"What? Like everyone in town doesn't know the story of the Cado Lake Massacre. I camp in those woods with my husband every summer and nothing's ever happened to us. In fact, I'm shutting down early tonight and taking a long weekend to go into those very woods."

"How early?" Ethan asked. He guzzled his beer and asked for another.

"In about half an hour I'm giving last call. Kitchen's shutting down now unless you boys have any last requests."

Henry's stomach turned to ice. The hand holding his beer trembled like a paint shaker. Slowly, so slowly, his eyes, feeling suddenly dry and huge, turned toward Dolly. She was still speaking, though Henry could hear nothing but ringing in his ears and the shrill shrieks coming down to him from nearly two decades past. Dolly smiled at him, but what Henry saw before him was a time-lapsed image of the psychotic girl in the carnival costume holding a knife to his groin.

Dolly would be the right age. Henry had always suspected the killers were locals. It had never occurred to him that those crazies could be people he knew, people he spoke to and interacted with daily. Henry peered around the room at all the regulars who despised him, searching their faces, watching their posture. It could be any of them. Even Ethan or Joel. How could he know? How could he keep Jack safe? How could he be certain if anybody he ever ran into was one of the four? How could he be certain of anything?

One thing he knew in that moment: Dolly had said "any last requests," and her voice was exactly how he'd remembered it for all these years.

Henry dropped a twenty on the bar. "That's it for me, then, guys. See you tomorrow."

"Where you off to?" Joel asked.

"Just heading home," Henry said. It wasn't true, and he was certain they knew it.

~

Jack finished erecting his tent and sat next to Mia on a log near the fire. Noah and Riley sat on the far side, their faces and bodies pressed together creating a flickering silhouette set against the darkening woods. Mia scooted close to Jack, leaned into him. It was clear what she wanted, but Jack was lost in thought, staring into the flames, sipping bitter beer from the bottle in his hand.

There was noise in the trees, crunching and cracking, and

Mia flinched, clinging against Jack.

"What is that?" she whispered.

"Just the woods," Jack said, as if he knew. Truth was, he'd never been camping. His father had never allowed it. He didn't have a clue what sounds were common in the woods. The night was full of chirping and hooting, alive with whistling and rustling. Before him, the fire popped and hissed. Beyond that, Noah and Riley smacked lips loudly, ignoring the world around them.

Mia looked about furtively, her big eyes turning up to Jack more than once. Then she seemed to forget what had frightened her and turned her attention back to s'more preparation.

A tall shadow leapt from beside Jack's tent and into the ring of firelight, shouting, "I'm Hatchett Henry and I'm here for my son!"

Mia shrieked. Both Jack and Noah were on their feet, ready to fight. Riley sat rigid on the blanket she and Noah had been seated on. Jack's hand went to the knife on his belt, but he didn't draw it. Recognition set in. It was just Caleb being an ass, thinking he was funny. He was tall and broad, a big kid growing into a big man. Jack thought Caleb had a way to go before he'd be all grown up.

High-pitched giggling followed Caleb from the shadows and Alexis strolled into the light. "Good one, babe."

"Yeah," Riley droned. "Real nice."

"Don't do that," Noah said, giving Caleb a rough shove.

"Were you worried I was him?"

"No. You just startled me, man." Caleb stood tall and proud, his smile flashing like the fire.

"You can relax," Jack said evenly, his words coming out in cool, controlled measures. He eyed Noah and Caleb hard. "My dad's not coming out here." He turned away from them and sat down next to Mia.

"I'm just messing with you, buddy." Caleb sauntered toward the long log and plopped down next to Jack, popped open a can, and began chugging beer. "Your dad's a local legend; it's nothing to be ashamed of."

"I'm not ashamed," Jack said.

"Can we just not talk about it?" Mia said.

"My dad doesn't have his own nursery rhymes," Caleb said. He handed his beer to Alexis and lit a cigarette. "I think it's cool."

"Well," said Jack, "it's not."

"He is famous." Noah shrugged noncommittally.

"Infamous," Riley corrected.

"Right," Noah said. "Same thing."

Giggling, dropping her voice an octave, pretty, blonde-haired Alexis stood in the light of the dancing flames and began chanting. "*One, Two, Henry lost a screw.*"

Caleb sang: "*Three, Four, they found him covered in gore.*"

"That's not right," Noah said. "It's *killed them as they snored.*"

Riley rose to her feet and slapped Noah in the back of his head.

"What the hell?" Noah said.

Jack couldn't stomach this. How could they be so cruel? He stood and stomped away from camp, heading into the forest.

"Wait," Mia said.

Jack strode away. Mia hurried after him.

"*Five, Six,*" Alexis raised her voice to the trees, "*at least he made it quick.*"

"*Seven, Eight, Henry mutilates.*" Jack could hear the elation in Noah's voice and that tone hurt the most. Noah was Jack's best friend, but he would ridicule Jack, mock him, join in this wicked, taunting slander of Jack's father with no regard to how it affected Jack. Jack couldn't get out of range fast enough.

Mia caught Jack's arm. "Wait, Jack. Please. Don't wander off in the dark."

"I can't listen to that. I thought it wouldn't bother me, but it does."

"I know it does," she said. "But I'm scared of the woods at night, and I don't want to be alone with them. Can't we just hang out in the tent? Just the two of us?"

Jack breathed deep. "I suppose you have a way to keep me distracted?"

Mia smiled. "I'll think of something."

~

The moon was high, and the night was warm. Knowing Jack, he was sleeping by now. The boy loved to sleep. Of course, it was possible he was out here with a girl. Henry wasn't ready to stumble upon that particular horror but

70

wasn't willing to turn back either. He needed to see that Jack was safe, even if that meant only spying on him from the cover of the trees. Henry would stand in the woods all night like a sentry if he needed to, but he would ensure Jack's safety no matter what anyone thought about it.

It wasn't hard to track the kids through the woods. Henry picked up their wide, clumsy trail starting where they'd parked their cars and was working his way into the forest. He didn't know what he'd do when he found them. It wasn't his intention to embarrass Jack, but there was a fear deep inside that drove Henry, a sense that danger was always lurking. Something evil could befall Jack at any moment and Henry would do whatever he could to prevent it.

~

Jack woke abruptly. There was someone there. Someone in the tent. He felt the warmth of Mia next to him, the gentle ebb and flow of her repose; but he felt another presence as well. He opened his eyes in the pitch darkness but saw nothing.

Reaching for his flashlight, Jack shone the beam up into the wicked face of a shiny plastic mask: the image of a furry wolf's face looking down at him. The man in the mask held a knife and rope.

"Time to go," the man said. "Grab him."

Three other figures entered behind the wolf: a witch, a skull, and a white, expressionless plastic face.

Strong hands took him by the ankles, dragged him from

the tent. He fought, kicking and swinging, but he was on his back, his feet held firmly, and before he knew what was happening Jack felt his body being set upright in a camping chair, the rope sliding around his body, binding his limbs to the chair.

He was near the fire. The flames burned the flesh of his arms and face. The smoke stung his eyes. Sweat began seeping from him. Beyond the flames, the four masked shadows were mere apparitions in the night.

Mia was pulled from the tent by her hair, screaming, then hogtied, gagged, and shoved face first into the dirt.

"What is this?" Jack said.

"Your past," Caleb said from behind the wolf mask. "Our past, coming to the present to haunt you."

"Retribution," said Riley.

"Your father lived that night," said the skull in a voice that sounded like Alexis.

"Mine did not," said the dead-eyed white face with the voice of Noah.

"Nor did mine," said Riley the witch.

"You're not from here," Jack said.

"No, I'm not. After your dad killed my dad, my mom took me away from this terrible town. But I'm back now."

"What do you want from me?"

"Justice," said Riley.

The wolf shook his head. "It's not about you, Jack. It's about making things right."

"Your dad took away people we love." The skull stepped

forward. "People we never got to love." The skull produced a knife much like the one on Jack's hip.

"Now," said Noah. "We've got to take away what he loves." Noah stepped into view, dragging an ax behind him through the dirt, the heavy head carving a winding, snakelike trail in the soft forest floor.

~

He could hear them up ahead, singing those damned nursery rhymes, tormenting Jack with them. A melody of male and female voices, taunting, jolly, singing

"Henry Hatchett at wit's end
Took an ax and killed his friends
Though they begged, he cut them down
Carved their faces into frowns"

Henry's guts twisted as he thought of Jack hearing that. He pushed forward through the undergrowth, pressing toward the flickering light in the distance, not knowing what he would do when he reached it, but thinking he might throttle some teenaged bastard for tormenting his son with those songs.

~

Jack was working a hand free behind him. Noah and Caleb were drunk and had done a poor job of tying Jack's hands. If he could keep them talking, he could get free and get away. But what about Mia? She lay there in the dirt, bound, gagged, awake and struggling. He saw the glisten of tears on her face, the smear of makeup. He couldn't leave her here; he'd have to fight his way to her and take her with him.

"You like that song?" Alexis taunted. "I've got one I made up on my own. Ready for it?" She danced away into the firelight, prancing a circle around Noah, who staggered drunkenly with the wood-handled ax propped on one shoulder.

"Hatchett Henry lost his mind
Bound his classmates up with twine
Poor little sister in her gown
He sunk an ax into her crown"

Alexis finished and began giggling maniacally.

As if on cue, Noah hefted the ax, turned and swung with all his strength down at Mia.

"NO!" Jack screamed. He hopped in his chair, finally managing to pull his right hand free, and toppled sideways nearly falling into the flames.

Mia rolled to one side, narrowly avoiding the head-splitting blow. The ax head sunk into the earth beside her. Frantically, she rolled her body away from Noah, but Riley was there to hold her steady.

Caleb was standing over Jack, swaying, reaching down to pull Jack back into a sitting position. "Where are you going?"

The bigger, stronger Caleb sat Jack up with little effort. Even when drunk, Caleb was an ox. Something gleamed in

Caleb's hand then: a steel hatchet he'd taken from a sheath at his hip. "Fitting, isn't it? A hatchet for Hatchett Henry's kid?"

Fear gripped Jack. Fear, and the need to survive, to escape, to save Mia. With his free hand, Jack tore the knife from its sheath at his hip and in one smooth motion he plunged it forward into Caleb's belly, then again into his chest, then a third quick stab upward into the bobbing Adam's apple beneath that grinning wolf's face.

Trembling, he cut the ropes that bound him and pounced from the chair. Skulled-faced Alexis was fleeing into the dark, but Noah and the witch were upon Mia. Jack lurched forward to stop the falling ax, but he was too far away to help, too late to save Mia.

As he watched the world slow around him, felt Caleb's blood slick on his hand, Jack saw a shadow leap through the air. A large body threw itself out into the night and collided with Noah. The ax clattered to the ground as the two tangled bodies tumbled into the darkness.

Riley went for the ax. Jack rushed forward, driving his fist into that wrinkled green mask. Riley toppled backward. Jack scrambled atop her, punching again and again until he was sure she was unconscious. He tore away her mask, needing to see the human face beneath the monster. She was bloodied, lips swelling, nose bent to one side and flattened. She would not be pretty again for some time.

Jack looked to Mia, who was tied and terrified, but otherwise seemed unharmed. He left her, grabbed the ax, and raced to the struggling figures in the darkness. The larger of the two had the other conquered, but as Jack approached Noah drew a small blade and plunged it into the belly of the larger man.

The big man stood, reeling, and stepped toward the light, one hand covering the wound in his belly.

"Dad?" Jack looked into Henry's eyes as Henry fell to one knee, breathless.

From the dark, Noah came forward, bloody blade in hand. Jack pulled the ax up behind him and over his head, driving the blade down into the white mask with a sickening thud. The ax head buried itself deep, stuck, and the handle was pulled from Jack's hands as his one-time friend toppled over, dead and twitching.

"Better untie the girl," Henry said between labored breaths. He held his belly tight with both hands.

"You're hurt."

"Better call me an ambulance, too."

~

Two days later Jack stood across the table from his father in the cutting room at Main Street Meats, a long, curved knife in his hand. "So, this is it?" Jack asked.

"Just that easy." Henry demonstrated the knife-wielding technique and removed meat from bone, wincing as he cut, the pain in his belly still fresh, still tender. "Always cut away from yourself."

"I mean," Jack motioned around the air-conditioned room. "This. We just move on, as if nothing happened?"

"Oh, it happened." Henry didn't look up but kept his eyes on his work. "You'll never forget it happened. But you move on." He shrugged. "Still got bills to pay. Debts don't care what you've been through. Still got to eat, sleep, live. You do what you have to. You get by."

"Just that easy?" Jack asked.

Henry looked up then, gazed across that red-stained table at his son. "Yeah," he said. "Just that easy."

Looking down at his work, Jack slid the sharp blade against the bone, separating the meat, trying not to think of the blood. Trying not to see the faces of the dead. "You ever think of leaving?"

Henry shrugged. "I've come to like this work."

"Not the job. Why'd you stay here all these years? Why not live somewhere else?"

"One place is as good as another, I suppose. Never really thought of it. My dad lived here, his dad. I grew up here. It was just always home."

"It doesn't feel like home to me," Jack said. "Never has."

"Where would you like to go?"

"Anywhere. Someplace where nobody knows us."

Henry put his knife down and looked at Jack. "You want me to go with you?"

"I want you to not live here, dad. I want you to be happy, to get away from your past."

"You can't outrun the past, Jack."

"Maybe you can dodge it," Jack said. He looked at the clock. It was nearly 4:00. "We could clean up, collect our pay, and leave tonight. Never look back."

Henry nodded slowly and wiped his hands on his apron. "If you think we can make a go of it, we'll move on. Maybe on the way, I'll tell you my story."

"Sure," Jack said. "And I'll tell you mine."

~~~

Notes on Henry Hatchett

A small press called A Murder of Storytellers *put out an anthology called* When the Sirens Have Faded. *The theme was, what happens to the survivors of horror movies? The task was to write about that survivor, that final girl, the one who made it out. What is her life like the next day, the following week, a decade later? How does this event affect those close to this survivor?*

Henry Hatchett was written with this in mind. Though this story was not accepted by A Murder of Storytellers, *I can proudly claim publication in* When the Sirens Have Faded. *My story* Shadows *appears there.*

Skittens

he came to the door one night wet thin beaten and
terrorized
a white cross-eyed tailless cat
I took him in and fed him and he stayed
grew to trust me until a friend drove up the driveway
and ran him over
I took what was left to a vet who said, "not much
chance...give him these pills...his backbone
is crushed, but is was crushed before and somehow
mended, if he lives he'll never walk, look at
these x-rays, he's been shot, look here, the pellets
are still there...also, he once had a tail, somebody
cut it off..."

Charles Bukowski
from *The History of One Tough Motherfucker*

Skittens

Day 1

The guards are monstrous, something like huge hairless cats. Bipedal, weird feline eyes the size of volleyballs, six-fingered hands with opposable thumbs, but they're cats all right. They don't respond when I hurl insults at them, beg to be set free, or ask questions. They don't seem to understand English, but they do speak amongst themselves. They wear uniforms like military personnel or maybe nurse's scrubs.

I don't have any clothes. None. They dropped me unceremoniously into this cage after roughly stripping me. Not sure what that's all about.

I don't know if they understand that I'm writing, but I keep myself hidden in a corner while I scrawl this. The cage is covered with a strange dark bedding much like pine shavings, but an indigo hue. When I pissed in the corner, my urine on this wood created a type of ink. A sliver of shaving serves as a quill of sorts. And the weird scratching post at the center of the cage is layers of crisp paper that can be peeled away.

Skittens

So, I'm keeping a journal written in urine. Yeah, it's gross, and it stinks, but it's all I've got.

Day 2

My name is Edward Finney. I live in New Mexico, not far from Roswell. I did, I mean, before I was taken. Now it seems I'm in a cage on a spacecraft. One of the huge cat-things opened the door to the cage today, scooped out the bedding I pissed on, scraped up my shit from one corner, and dropped some strange tablets into a bowl.

The tablets are meant to be food. They're big and I have to nibble pieces off. Not surprisingly, they taste like chicken.

Day 3

There's a giant water bottle on the front of my cage, like the one my gerbil used to have. The silver tube has a little nipple at the end that makes me wish for some female company. What can I say? I'm bored and lonely.

Day 4

My captors seem to be able to read my mind. Today a woman was brought to my cage. She is tall, blond, pretty and doesn't speak a lick of English. Maybe I can teach her.

Oh, and she's naked, which is nice. Very nice. She's got hair in places I'm unaccustomed to seeing hair on women, but I'm not going to say anything. I mean, she hasn't said anything about my smell, and at this point I must be ripe.

I'm staring at the beautiful naked stranger when it hits

me: I don't even know her name.

Day 9

Her name is Marta and she is from Norway. She's picked up English quickly. Turns out she did know some, but that day they'd thrown her in here, the cat had got her tongue. Literally. They'd given her some kind of rough teeth-cleaning that had left her tongue swollen and her throat miserable. Marta started talking yesterday.

She's been here among the Skittens for about a month. Skittens means space kittens. Marta came up with that. They took her from just outside Lillehammer and tossed her in a cage, like they did me. But on her second day, one of them pulled her out and held her in its arms, squeezing her to its thin chest while stroking her hair alternately softly and roughly. She says it was most unpleasant and went on for hours. The more Marta squirmed and kicked, hissed and screamed, the tighter the grip became, the rougher the petting.

"What did they do then?" I asked her.

"Put me back in the cage."

Day 13

The paper I'm writing on is the shredded remains of a tall cylinder in the center of our room. Each day I pull strips off it and each day the outer sheath of paper is replaced with a new smooth layer of paper. It seems to please the captors that we do this.

Skittens

As I write this, today, Marta has been taken away and is being cuddled once more. I can see her from where I'm at, being held against the pale orange flesh of a Skitten. They wear clothes, and their faces betray no hint of gender.

The Skitten touched Marta in a way she didn't like. I heard her cry out, and say, "Stop!" but the stupid creature kept jostling her. Marta reached out and scratched the Skittens cheek and, with a second batting hand she got it in the blue-gold eye. The beast wrapped its six-fingered clawed hand around Marta's slim frame and squeezed until she stopped kicking.

They've taken her away. I don't know if she's alive or dead.

Day 14

A day and night have passed and no sign of Marta. I do hope she comes back.

I've been provided a wheel to climb. It's like a hamster wheel, but huge. I'll admit I was bored enough to spend the better part of the afternoon trying to climb one side of it.

Day 15

Still no Marta.

They brought me a new type of food today, some sort of juicy meat. I try not to think of what it might be. It's been a while since I've had meat.

Day 17

I have a new cellmate today. She's pretty enough, but she's no Marta. I'm beginning to think Marta isn't coming back. I haven't talked to this one yet. She's been hiding in a corner, burrowing into bedding and sobbing since they dropped her in my cage.

I've learned two things about this new woman. Her name is Erica and these monsters have cut off each finger at the first knuckle. She, like Marta, struck out at one of the Skittens, cutting his furless flesh with her long nails. We haven't learned their language, but she and I agree that this mutilation was done in retaliation for her clawing the beast's face.

Without the first knuckle of her fingers, Erica's nails will never grow back. I'm certain the same thing has been done to Marta. I'm beginning to understand the purpose these creatures have for us and I'm truly frightened.

Day 18

Never thought I'd say it. I miss Roswell.

Day 21

Erica's fingers have healed. Each now ends in a stub, but the wounds are closed. At night, when I'm trying to sleep, I can hear her sobbing and licking her fingers.

Day 25

Erica and I have become close. She sleeps near me, her

warm body pressed to mine, her long hair twining into mine.

We stink less. Erica cleans up nicely. She's much prettier than I first thought. We've found a way to bathe by spraying water from the rubber nipple into a small recess in one of the toys they gave us.

Yes. Toys.

They've given us balls to push around with little bells inside of them and a number of other demeaning things. We have something round and flat, and we don't know its purpose, but we use it for a Frisbee and for bathing.

Day 29

I made love to Erica last night. It's the closest I've felt to normal since my abduction. She tried scratching my back, but that just led to more sobbing.

Day 32

One of the guards caught me screwing Erica and pulled me out of the cage. Its feline face was ferociously close to me, my arms trapped at my side as it held me in a tight six-fingered grip. Skitten spittle sprayed me as it roared in my face. Of course, I didn't understand a single word—the stupid creature doesn't seem to understand I don't speak its language. It went on and on, raging at me, shaking me, squeezing me. I got the message though: he was pissed. But why? They've paired us male and female. Do they not want us to mate?

C. L. Phillips

Day 39

They do not want us to mate. After the lashing I took from the angry guard, I guess I should have known sex was off limits. But I'm bored, okay? So bored. I mean, you take a male and female of any species and put them together with nothing else to do, what do you think they are going to do?

But they've fixed that now. I won't be banging anything for a long, long time. Probably never again.

They took me away from the cage a few days ago. I could sense something bad coming, so when they reached in for me, I cowered near the back of the cage. That only incensed them. One of them (I really can't tell them apart) finally managed to snatch me up after going elbow-deep into the cage. He cut his arms on the sharp wires and took it out on me. I was slapped left and right, then knocked sprawling as this enraged Skitten grabbed me by the head.

I sat my ass down, the way a dog does when he's playing keep away, and I threw all my weight away from the six clawed fingers. This only hurt me. I slipped, fell back, clunked my head, and was dragged out by two sharp claws digging into my calves.

Part of me expected Erica to come to my aid. Another part of me understood why she didn't. What was she going to do, dig at them with her finger stumps?

I kicked and punched, clawed and bit, but I was no match for my assailant. He was easily three times my size. Probably much more. These weird cat-things are huge, I'm telling you. If anyone ever reads this, you'll probably have encountered these bastards and you'll already know. On the off chance this handmade notebook makes it to Earth, or to humans at any rate, you should know we're not alone in the universe and some of the other races are assholes.

~

I couldn't bring myself to tell this part earlier, but now that I'm rested and healing, Erica says writing it down will be therapeutic.

They shoved me in a small plastic box and carried me through the ship. In a small room, they laid me down on a cold metal table beneath a hot, blinding light. A thin membranous sheet was pulled up over my body by two Skittens, one on either side of me. They were dressed differently than the others, wearing white gowns. One of them flipped a switch on a panel. The heat intensified and the sheet began to shrink like that plastic stuff northern people put on their windows in winter. It began molding itself to my body, pulling me down, pressing me tight against the table. Only my head was free. They didn't bother with that.

Lifting my head, I watched as they went to work.

When one of them came at my midsection with a wickedly curved, shining scalpel, I began to scream. "Wait a minute! What are you doing?" To them I must sound the way dogs or pigs sound to us. So, they went about their business as if I weren't even there.

They ignored my screams.

A chill ran through me as cool air rushed in upon my

crotch. Every muscle clenched as a firm hand rubbed at my equipment with cold gel. I mean, in hindsight, this would make the perfect Kegel exercise. The other Skitten took something from a nearby tray and my heart pumped furiously as I recognized it from my early farm days. Those poor fucking pigs. Finally, after all these years, I'm learning to empathize.

The vigorous application of the gel ended—in any other situation, this attention paid to my unit would have been appreciated—and the applicant grabbed my shaft and pulled it roughly up toward my belly. I was trapped, my body motionless. My head swung back and forth so hard, so fast, I was giving myself whiplash. My neck ached, and I began getting lightheaded.

It would have been best if I'd passed out then, but I did not.

With a single, deftly skilled motion the rubber band went around my scrotum, way up high against my pelvis. The beast released it with a *snap,* and I squealed like a pig.

I lay there weeping, screaming, struggling against the tight sheet, all to no avail. The Skitten surgeons left the room and didn't come back for two days. After that, they came in and made one swift cut to remove my balls and gave me a few stitches for the bleeding.

A tube was shoved down my throat for food and water. I was left two more days for healing before being brought back to Erica.

Skittens

Day 41

I've been taken off-ship and moved into the private quarters of a Skitten family. Erica is not with me. There is no sign of other human life.

Day 43

I'm beginning to see slight differences in the Skittens. This family has two young: a male and female. It seems that I am the pet of the female. The male enjoys tormenting me to hurt her. Today, he took me out and put me on the floor, as if to let me explore. He kept me corralled between his enormous feet, directing my movements, leading me into another room. I can't see much from the floor. Their furniture is huge. Mostly it looks like an Earth home, which is weird. Anyway, he kept me out of the cage all day and when the female came home, the male swatted me until I pissed all over myself and on the floor. Then he rubbed my nose in it and made her watch.

Day 47 (I think)

I'm not sure how long I've been away from Roswell now. Away from Earth. I try to count sleep cycles, but I lose track. Most of my time is spent napping or listening to the fearful beating of my heart.

Day 51

I have a new companion, John. He's taller than I am, dark haired, and he still has his balls. This matters more than

I wish it did.

Day 52

John is dominant.

Day 54

They gave us a female today. Gloria. She's got smooth brown skin and midnight black hair. Her eyes are dark too. She looks at me with disdain.

Day 58

For three days I watched John and Gloria screw. In this new home, it is allowed. The Skittens won't cut his balls off. They want these humans to breed.

Gloria has begun looking at me with pity. She's become kind and even speaks to me. Yesterday, after they were through, she sat and shared a meal with me. Of course, this angered John and he attacked me.

Maybe he's not so dominant after all. I beat the shit out of him. Guess balls aren't everything.

Day 59

This female I belong to, the daughter in this strange alien family, she's got her favorites and I don't count among them. She's given me to the male child.

He hasn't fed me today.

Skittens

Day 61

No sign of the male Skitten. I've been alone in this dark cage for many days. Squinting, I write this by the soft light coming in from the big window over his low bed.

Day 63

The mother Skitten found me today, half-starved, weak, and dying. I still don't understand their language, but anger sounds the same on every planet. She must be a pet-lover. She gave me food and water and lit into the child something fierce. Then she left me alone with him.

Day 65

He put a large creature in with me. Something like a rat/spider. Furry and fuzzy all over, with many horrible eyes and a weird, gnawing mouth that moves as its nose twitched. It was horrifying and meant to kill me. Kill me slowly, I think. The thing didn't come near, though, but kept a wary distance as if it were afraid of me.

The cruel Skitten grew bored of our defensive dance and removed the creature after some time.

I've spent the better part of today alone in the dark, thinking of the thing that frightened me and was frightened by me. Where does it come from? What do they call it? I don't know where I am, what world I'm on, or whether I'm in the same galaxy or universe as Earth. Does the rat/spider come from the world of the Skittens or from another world? Are they collecting species from planets the way humans gather creatures from around the world to put in zoos, to keep as pets?

Am I now part of an interstellar menagerie?

Day 68

After failing to kill me with the monstrous visitor, the young male Skitten has packed me up in a box and taken me away. I find myself in yet another cage of similar design: wire walls, a glass or plastic top that I can't reach, hamster wheel, woodchip bedding, water dispenser with nipple, big food dish filled with pellets. There are many humans in this cage with me. They were all here before me. Some are American, others British or Australian.

Thank God. At least we can talk to each other.

Just when I was beginning to think the Skittens had somehow segregated us by language, I learned that two men speak Cantonese. One woman speaks Egyptian, another French, and yet another Somali. Among them, the French and Somali women are linguists and have begun deciphering some of the Skitten language.

This is welcome news, and I ask them to teach me. The French woman, Giselle, agrees to share what she knows, though she promises me I won't like it.

Day 70

Giselle has begun teaching me the scratching Skitten tongue and I'm sorry I asked her to. I can catch a word now that I didn't know two days ago: Specimen. We are in a laboratory.

According to Giselle and Sabrina, the Somali woman, who both speak fluent English, we are the unwanted pets who have been sent off to the pound. This pound is a drug-testing facility. They assure me that no one has left the huge sterile room alive and whole. If I leave, I will be blind, deaf, mutilated, irradiated, or dead.

"Probably all of those," Sabrina says before making her way back to the food dish, her hips swaying in a way that no longer appeals to me.

Day 72

Two men were added to our cage today. One is deaf, the other blind. The blind man is Jonas and he's got a rash all over his body. He's been neutered too, and even this area is puckered and red. They slathered an ointment on him. "It burned immediately," he tells us, "but the screaming didn't stop them. The four of them just stood there, watching me writhe, marking notes on clipboards and tapping keyboards. It was inhumane."

"What does he expect?" Giselle asks me when we're alone in one corner. "They're not human."

I can't help but wonder if we are still human, those of us who think we are.

Day 77

My name is Giselle Le Roux. I write this day in place of my friend, Edward Finney. He likes to be called Eddie, but now he wants to be left alone. The beasts the Americans have named Skittens took him to their testing facility. Before any tests could be performed, he lashed out and leapt from the arms of the one who held him. It will be many days before Eddie is able to hold the wood shavings we use as writing utensils. As has happened to many of us, his fingertips have been removed.

Beyond that, his legs have been broken. A barbaric thing these animals do to prevent those who would flee.

Day 81

Giselle again. It was my intention to continue writing for Eddie as long as he desired to continue this journal. I don't know how he managed to keep it with him as he was moved from place to place, but I am afraid to try.

Edward Finney died during a Skitten experiment. One of the others saw him convulse and fall still. His body was taken to an incinerator.

Day 85

I heard the Skittens speak of short supply. They intend to return to Earth for further collection of specimens. This will be the final entry in this journal by my hand. It is my hope that it will help others. I pray it finds you well.

~~~

Notes on Skittens

This story was a long time coming.

I don't call myself an animal lover. I don't dislike them, I'm just

Skittens

not much for keeping pets and caring for them. It has always appalled me that people who do claim that title—animal lover—do things to their pets that seem, to me, to be very cruel. I am thinking, of course, of neutering, declawing, forced breeding, and the like.

Skittens *marinated in the back of my mind for years. At last, I think I found the right format for it and wrote it down.*

High Steaks

When I saddle the pale horse, to take my last ride,
To the home ranch, over the Great Divide,
Will I find the trail blazed all the way,
A place to camp, at the close of day?

James W. Whilt
from *The Pale Horse*

High Steaks

For the most part there was dead silence. When anyone did speak, it was short and to the point: *Drink?* Words that didn't mean anything, didn't carry any weight. A canteen or bottle would pass by the fire, pass back to where it had come from. The stillness of dusk was heavier than any conversation the four of us could rustle up. In that calm quietness on the open dusty range, words passing between us were just more noise in the background.

We were four men sitting together in a little grove of pine and aspen atop a hill overlooking a long stretch of land where cattle were supposed to be grazing. But there were no cattle. Just emptiness spread out under the dimming sky.

A horse whinnied and shook its mane. A boot caught a rock and sent it rolling. The empty ring of tin on tin as coffee was poured out into a small cup. Empty sounds in an empty land. Before us was the night, the range, and the mystery of nearly one hundred missing head. Here, in the camp with us, was the stillness of men, the empty meaninglessness of their words: *Coffee? Beans? Jerky?* And the following grunt that somehow meant less as a shadowy hand stretched forth to take the proffered provision.

Three men sat around the dwindling fire, waiting for the flames to die. The fourth stood against a tree watching the sunlight fade in the distance, his eyes following a light grey outline that moments before had been a black speck on the long horizon. I watched Silas straighten and knew Charlie had returned. He'd found something. No way Charlie would have come back if he hadn't grabbed hold of something useful.

From the fire, we watched Silas Stubbs step away from the tree, the faded denim of his coat stretched tight across his shoulders, across his broad back. I'd followed that denim coat across a lot of miles the past few days, looking at the back of the boss as he led us out here, to the place of the missing cattle.

We'd been in a saloon, eating steaks and drinking whiskey, when the tale came in. An old-timer in a weathered hat slurped beer as he laid out the story before us. He was a rancher, I reckoned, looking to hire cowboys to track down what was left of his herd. A few beef cattle were found tore up on the range. The rest were missing. "No animal done this," the old-timer had said. "It was men, or savages." I wanted to tell the old man that savages were men too, but I'd sat quiet, as is my wont, and let Silas do the talking. Silas was the boss. Talking was his place, not mine. I just sat quiet with Charlie, Davie, and the Kid, chewing on the best steak I'd had in some time, waiting for Silas to decide, waiting to find out if I had work coming.

"We're not cow punchers," Silas had told the man. He was careful to not say what it was we were. "But if there's a bounty, we'll hunt it."

"Three dollars a head, is what I can offer," the old man had said.

"Point us in the direction," Silas said between drinks. "We'll catch 'em and bring 'em back."

Four days later I was sitting by a fire, watching the night close in, waiting for Silas to tell us when to pack up and head out.

The horse came to a stop as Silas took its reins and Charlie Mims swung down from his saddle, stretched his arms over his head, twisted from side to side to relieve the stiffness. "Whole herd's been pushed west, across the river. Trail's easy enough to pick up." He moved past Silas, and made his way toward the fire, looking down at me and Davie and the Kid. "Coffee?"

I poured him a tin and handed it over. Charlie drank, staring into the flames. Suppose he'd said all he thought was necessary, but I watched Silas following Charlie Mims with his eyes, the same question lingering there.

"Who took them?"

"Can't say," Charlie said.

"But the trail's warm?"

"Warm as this fire, Silas. Can't move a hundred cows without leaving a trail."

"First light," Silas said.

"First light," Davie said, answering for us all.

High Steaks

I grunted assent and turned in, rolling away from the fire and pulling my coat up over my head. Leave it to Davie or the Kid to douse the flames; and leave the talking to Charlie and the boss.

~

At first light, Silas Stubbs broke the silence of the night. "Mount up."

We were off and heading across the range, following Charlie Mims to where the herd had stomped its way into the shallows of the muddy river. It was sunup by the time we got there, and it was plain to see that Charlie had called it true. A lot of cattle had plunged into the river here and made their way across, no mistake. The far side was just as tore up.

"Can cows swim?" the Kid asked. He was young, maybe fourteen. None of us knew who his pa was, or his ma for that matter. Not that it made no difference. He was one of us now.

"Yeah," I said. "They swim pretty good."

We weren't much for talking, none of us. This seemed like a lot of words first thing in the day. Not so much words, because words have meaning. Mostly we grunted phrases or kept quiet. The sun was coming up fast, pushing the clouds out of the way so it could fall full on us, burning the sand and dirt and scrub. It was too bright to focus. I couldn't see the tracks Charlie was following, so I rode next to the Kid, just ahead of Davie, and followed Charlie and the boss.

"Will we hang 'em?" the Kid asked.

"We'll hang 'em," Silas said from atop his horse.

"What about the law?" Davie asked. He'd been a slave before the war, and didn't like to hear no talk of hanging, no matter the reason.

"Law says cattle rustlers hang," Silas called back.

I looked at the Kid and back at Davie. They were thinking what I was thinking: sheriffs do the hanging. But I was also thinking along lines with Silas and Charlie; no way was I dragging rustlers with us while we were driving stolen cattle back to its rightful owner. Rustlers can swing from any tree. No need to drag them to town.

"If we find the cows and drive them back," the Kid said, "what happens if we get caught with them? Do we get hung for rustlin'?"

I looked back at Davie. He looked sick. Him and me, we'd seen too many folks hang.

"Nah," Charlie said. "We got papers from the owner."

"Nobody's hanging me," said Silas Stubbs. "Never."

We rode on in silence for some time, which is the way I prefer it. A stink came up, something foul floating off the river. Swatting a sudden swarm of flies away, I fell back behind the others. In the distance, something huge roared, like a beast I'd never heard in these parts; and off beyond that roar, the sound of a stampede, the rush of a hundred hooves pounding the earth to beat hell.

"Indians?" I called up ahead.

"Apache," Charlie threw back.

"War party?" I checked my six-shot, made sure it was

loaded, then holstered it and took up my Winchester. They say it won the West. I just needed it to win the day.

"Hunters," Silas said. His voice was low, his head high, searching the horizon.

"Coming this way?" I asked him.

"Get up here and see."

The others had stopped atop the hill and I rode up beside them, looking down over the wide prairie. Away off, the mountains stood to the north and west. Nearer, the river twisted to the west, disappearing from sight before it ran into the mountains. Coming across the other way, like they was fleeing the sun itself, was a band of two dozen Indians riding bareback on skinny horses, chasing a herd of cattle.

"Those our cows?" Davie asked.

"I reckon," Silas said. He spit a black wad of tobacco.

"I'm telling you," Charlie said, "I think ours was already pushed through that river."

"Smells like some of them died," the Kid put in.

Down below, the Indians ran on in silence, pushing their horses after the moving herd. Not far off, little piles of meat sat beneath buzzing mounds of flies. The tore-up cows we'd been told of, I reckoned. The wind brought that stink full in my face. On that wind, a rushing, roaring noise poured down from heaven, coming closer every second. "What is that?" I asked.

"Twister, maybe," Charlie said.

"Ain't never heard no twister like that," Davie said.

"No." Silas's voice was fading as his eyes followed the

Apache rustlers. "That's no twister."

"Then what?" I pressed.

Silas shrugged, the denim jacket shifting up and down in a single smooth motion. "Can't rightly say, boys. Maybe one of them Apache gods." His voice was the same as ever: serious.

Just then, as if Silas had summoned this Indian god, something big burst through the clouds, trailing fire from its behind. Long and smooth like a bullet, shining like copper, it swooped like the Thunderbird the Indians said roamed the skies. I'd never believed those tales of gods and monsters, but here before my own eyes was something from legend diving from the heavens, toward the earth. It went low, hovering not far above the cattle and the Indians. A bright light poured down from the beast, and the horses, Indians, and cows started coming off the ground, caught up like dry leaves on a cool breeze. When it rose again, many of the cattle and horses and Apaches were gone, swallowed up in the thing's belly.

"By God," Charlie murmured.

"Can you hang them rustlers?" the Kid asked.

"Shut up," Silas told him. "Come on. Still got our cattle to find."

"What was that?" Davie asked. His voice shook like the ground beneath a stampede. No one answered him.

The boss spurred his horse forward, flowing downhill and curving left toward the river. We followed in line like ants. I can't speak for the others, but my heart was going like a chicken's leg, just pumping and beating and working its way up my throat. Going forward into the realm of the Thunderbird seemed mighty stupid to me. I'd have much rather turned around and gone back to the camp, or further on to the town. If we never went after those cattle, never collected that three hundred dollars, it wouldn't make no difference. I was willing to leave it behind and move on. But the boss led us forward, following at a safe pace behind the Indians the Thunderbird had not swallowed up.

Those Apache turned upriver, fleeing alongside the cattle they were chasing. The boss didn't pay them no more heed. We crossed over the river, swimming alongside the horses, then stopped a spell to build a fire and dry our clothes. Nobody mentioned the Thunderbird, the cattle. Nothing. We sat in silence, like normal, only this time I could feel the fear shooting through each of us.

Over a can of beans, Silas said, "Charlie. Take Davie with you and go up yonder. See if you can pick up a clear trail or spot our quarry." His voice was still, calm, like he ain't seen nothing unusual.

"You heard the boss, Davie." Charlie sounded weary, but he wouldn't naysay Silas. "Mount up."

They rode off toward the west, promising to return by dusk. At dusk, the Kid and I set to playing cards and cooking bacon. Silas sat against a stone, drinking whiskey and watching the night come on. When the moon rose high and I dozed off, Charlie and Davie had not come back.

~

"Mount up," Silas said.

It was dawn. Barely any light was peeking up beyond the horizon. There were only three of us then. Charlie and Davie were gone.

"Did that monster take them?" the Kid was all eyes in the dim morning. His voice was shaky, the way you get when fear grabs you tight. Looking at him, I wasn't sure he'd slept a wink.

"Don't know," Silas said. "We'll track 'em. Track the cattle. Suppose we'll know soon enough."

"Reckon we will," I said. "Coffee?"

"Brew it fast. Breakfast too, if you need it. I want to get out ahead of the sun."

Hardtack, beans, and burnt coffee. Not my best meal, but it filled me. Neither the boss nor the Kid complained none, neither. By the time half the sun was up over the far trees, we were on horseback, following Silas as he followed the trail left by Charlie and Davie.

In my gut, I knew they were dead. Indians got 'em. Or that sleek metal beast, shining like the Lord's own glory. Or maybe the devil himself or something else. Didn't matter none. I knew they was dead, and I knew we was next. I wanted something desperate to turn back and forget about these cattle. They weren't my cows, and no cut of three hundred dollars was worth losing my hide over. But Silas pushed on, set on finding our boys and finding those cows and getting us that money. He was the boss, and I suppose he felt some responsibility for us, some kinship to us, like he was the patriarch of our small family.

We were a small gang. Never robbed a coach or stuck up a bank. Never drove cattle; never stole 'em neither. We were simple men, outcasts, leftovers from the war between the states. Each of us come out west to find a simple life on the open land, but things being what they are, and life being hard and dangerous for a man alone, we band together like brothers, chasing bounties, doing odd jobs, earning a few dollars here and there, when the work was reasonable. The prospect of three hundred divided five ways was mighty fine; but the true risk of life and limb wasn't what I'd call reasonable.

Still, Silas Stubbs was the man we called boss, so if he pressed on toward the land of the Thunderbird, I'd follow him. What else was I going to do?

About noon, we crested a hill and came on a herd of cattle marked with the brand we'd been searching for. Weren't no hundred of them. More like fifty or so, but it was them what we set out for. They roamed easy like, eating scrub and bending to drink from a slow brook ebbing down from the hills.

Something like a mound of shining copper, very much like that Thunderbird we'd seen yesterday, sat hunched up on that hill, and below it, bore into the side of the low rocky hills, was a wide cave.

"Horse tracks come right up here," Silas said. "Our boys are inside."

"Why'd they stay here?" I asked. "Why not come back

to camp and tell us what they found?"

"Don't know," Silas said. He dismounted and pulled his own Winchester from his saddle holster. Without another word, he moved on toward the cave.

The Kid looked at me, his eyes big and dry. I don't think he blinked once in the time it took to climb down from our mounts, check our guns, and trail after Silas.

That same stink that had come on me yesterday, just before the Thunderbird came from the clouds, that stink wafted from the cave mouth, sitting like a foul fog. I knew we'd have to plunge into that smell, but I didn't want to. That's the truth.

"What do we do?" the Kid whispered.

"Find our boys. Hang the rustlers." Silas spat tobacco and stepped forward, rifle in hand.

The Kid looked up at that squat monster on the hill, its body gleaming like polished brass in the midday sun. "These rustlers might not hang easy."

"Most don't," I said. "Come on now. Keep that gun ready."

The cave was not dark. I couldn't find the source of light, but the whole place was lit up like a church on Christmas. The walls weren't typical stone, but seemed to be coated with something shiny, smooth, like I was in a tunnel of steel. The smell of blood and offal rose up all around us and I was reminded of my uncle's slaughterhouse. He'd wanted me to work for him, but that type of work weren't for me. I retched, and Silas shot me a glance, his eyes telling me to man up. The Kid took it all in stride, as if the scent of death didn't affect him none.

We wound and descended, heading deeper into the earth. I didn't know if Silas was still tracking or just walking. As for me, I never looked at my feet, but kept my eyes peeled, ears keen, searching for a sign of men.

"Cattle come down this way," Silas said. "Kicked up dirt and dropped shit all along here. Horses too."

"Men?" the Kid asked.

"Maybe. And something else. Something I ain't seen before."

The Kid looked at me. I could only shrug. Silas was twice my age and had seen more of the world than I had. If there was something he hadn't seen before, I had no answers for the Kid.

A sound like steel scraping on steel came up the tunnel. Quick, rapid movements of *slink slink slink*. The noise was familiar, as if from an old dream, or a memory long forgotten. The buzzing of flies, millions of them swarming, echoed up the stone walls.

"What's that?" the Kid asked.

"You ask a lot of questions," Silas said. He put his rifle to his shoulder and moved ahead slowly.

The iron stench of blood was thick here. We'd come upon a heap of cow hides and piles of guts. Amid the brown and white of the fur, the pink and red of the innards, was the fluttering black of flies like a dense cloud in the pale light, and beneath that cloud, a slow-creeping blanket of white worms feasting on days-old rot.

Silas's dirty looks be damned: I vomited and turned back.

"Get that out," he said. "But you ain't leaving. Our boys are in here, and so is our reward."

I purged everything I'd eaten the past two days and, stepping around the charnel remains, followed Silas and the Kid deeper still. My eyes stung and blurred. My skin crawled beneath the touch of the flies. Still, I pushed forward, fearing now what had become of Charlie and Davie.

Having trouble seeing and breathing, I fell behind, losing sight of the others. It wasn't long though before I heard Silas's voice boom with authority.

"We're underground," he said, "but you go ahead and reach for the sky all the same."

When I caught up to him, Silas and the Kid both had drawn down on a huge man. The man was hairless, his ears pointed like a dog's, and he held a bloody knife above his head. He was shirtless, wearing only a leather apron and a chain belt, from which hung a sharpening steel like my uncle the butcher always had on hand, used to keep that butchering blade sharp. The skin was a pale green, scaled. This was no man. It was a creature like I'd never heard of. All I could see was its back and the smooth gleam of its bald, scaled head. Not a man, not a snake, not like anything God put on this Earth.

"He's got four arms," I said, the words slipping out quick, before my mind registered what that meant. My hands were shaking, my knees knocking. I was ready to shoot this thing full of holes; just waiting on word from the boss.

"A demon," the Kid whispered. I couldn't tell if his rifle or his voice had more shake, but both were quivering something terrible.

"Put that knife down, son," Silas commanded the demon. "Nice and easy." He was awful calm for a man holding a gun to a demon. I suppose Sam Colt gives a man unnatural courage.

Me, holding my Winchester steady at the four-armed thing's back, I was shaking fit to bring the cave tumbling down.

The demon lowered two of its arms slow-like, the muscles in its back and shoulders flexing weirdly, and put the knife and a thick-bladed cleaver on the strange gruesome workbench in front of it. When I mustered the strength to look away from the demon, letting my eyes take in the scene around me, I was sick all over again. Hooks had been placed along the cave ceiling and from them hung the bodies of cows and horses, and further down, the flayed corpses of men, headless, swinging from their ankles. So many men. Mostly Indians, was my guess, but I was certain that Charlie and Davie hung there too. When you take away the skin, men are the same underneath. Wish we'd thought of that before the war. I couldn't speak, couldn't think straight. This thing had butchered men, cut up my friends like sides of beef.

"He did like you said, Silas," said the Kid.

"Mighty wise, friend."

"He understands us, I mean, boss."

"Yes," said the demon. Its voice was deeper than the river valley, richer than a gold vein. "I have learned your language."

"What are you?" the Kid asked.

The creature breathed a long, deep breath before answering. "I am what you would call a chef."

"Where are you from?" I asked, finding my voice. My trigger finger was feeling heavy and my guts were heaving.

"Another world," the demon said. "Beyond the stars."

"What do you want?"

"Good steak," said the demon. "I have travelled far for many years, searching for the perfect meat. Many worlds have been hunted dry; the stores of creatures have run low. Your world is rife with life, a variety of tasty morsels. But here, I've found something that does not appear elsewhere in the universe."

"Men?" I asked.

"You're eating people?" the Kid said.

The demon shrugged, its four massive shoulders moving like small boulders. It turned to face us, lowering its hands. Its face was like a man's, but scaled; its mouth stretched in four directions, opening like one of them folded paper cranes paper things the Asians sell in the markets. Its eyes were slanted, narrow slits like a cat's. Its teeth, like needles.

"Hands to heaven, friend," Silas said. He was treating this creature as if it were any common rustler, as if it was human. I wondered then and I wonder now, if Silas saw this thing the same way I did, or if he'd been listening when it said it was from another world. Didn't seem to faze him at all. The boss was so set on the pay, it was like he'd shut off all his senses.

The creature raised its hands again. It must have had some sense of what a gun was. "I have found here, on this planet, the best steaks I've ever eaten."

"You don't mean beef steak, do you?" the Kid asked. He was looking sick again.

"No," the demon said. It smiled wickedly, then lunged toward Silas, taking the boss in the throat with a knife. Four hands are too many to keep eyes on.

I fired with my Winchester, but the demon was cat-quick, and pulled Silas between us. My bullet took the boss in the chest. The Kid fired, but his shot went wide.

The demon pushed the body of Silas aside and came on, pouncing. It must have thought me the next great threat, because it was hurtling through the air and nearly to me when the Kid let out a second shot, this one knocking the demon out of the air. I worked the lever of my Winchester furiously, firing from the hip, unloading every round into the monster's body, the Kid firing everything he had. When the rifle ran out, I drew Sam Colt and put six bullets into that weird, scaled head.

I'm not sure when the thing quit moving, but when the smoke cleared, it was so riddled with bullets it was nothing but a pile of meat for the flies and their young. I looked at the Kid and the Kid looked at me. We'd said enough words for this day, so silently, we stepped around the demon, past Silas, through the mess of charnel madness and made our way back out into the daylight.

Outside, we breathed the clean air and stared up at the sleek Thunderbird on the hill.

"What do we do now?" the Kid asked.

"Don't know. Reckon we should drive these cattle back and take the reward. What do you say?"

"Hell, no," the Kid said. "I don't ever want to see no damn cow again."

"Yeah," I said. "Me neither."

"What then?"

"California?"

"For what?"

"Gold," I said.

The Kid nodded. "Probably no demons from other worlds ever gonna come looking for gold."

"Probably not," I agreed. "Let them have their steaks. Can't be no danger in hunting gold."

We saddled up and headed west, not once looking back at the cattle or to the cave or to the strange metal bird perched on that hill.

When the sky thundered with that strange sound, and the earth shook beneath the force of the metal thing taking flight, the Kid looked at me and I looked back at the Kid, but neither of us turned to watch the strange Indian god from some other world flying. We'd seen enough. It was time to push on, leave the range behind, and seek our fortune in gold.

It seemed a safer path.

~~~

<u>Notes on High Steaks</u>

High Steaks *was published in* Reach for the Sky, *a weird western anthology from* Rogue Blades Entertainment. *It's the wild west meets science fiction. I've made my living as a butcher for many years now and, on occasion, someone will ask me if my butchering work has ever worked its way into my fiction. Well, until this story it had not.*

The Dismissal Song

What shall I your true love tell,
Earth-forsaking maid?
What shall I your true love tell
When life's spectre's laid? …

"Tell him, with speech at strife,
For last utterance saith:
'I who loved with all my life,
Loved with all my death.'"

Francis Thomson
from What shall I your true love tell

The Dismissal Song

"You have the heart?" the witch asked me.

I couldn't respond. My stomach roiled and churned. I held the awful bag of offal in my outstretched hand but felt no control over my movements. It was as if I was watching the scene from outside myself. I was sure of one thing only now: I'd lost all control of the situation.

The witch took the bag and dumped the heart onto the cutting board.

We were in her apartment, a small two-bedroom place on the ground floor of the Bluegrass Hills apartment complex on the banks of the Bluegrass River. It was kind of a nice place. Still, I loathed this apartment building almost as much as the deed that had brought that heart into my possession. Yeah, murder. I admit to it. But you don't understand, he had to die so that she could live. Or so I believed at the time. I wish it had not been my lot to kill him.

"You cut it out while he was alive, right?" the witch asked. She was not an old hag like the wart-nosed crone from Snow White. The witch I was involved with was a beautiful girl of nineteen, with straight brown hair and wide blue eyes. Her name was Tess, and she was the best friend of my fiancé, Liz. "It's important that you bring me a heart that was beating when it was removed, Joe, or the spell won't work."

I swallowed down bile. "Yes," I said.

"What? Speak up, man."

"Yes," I repeated. "He was alive."

"Good," she said. "Now set that table the way I showed you. I'll cut the heart."

Tess had one of those big, round kitchen tables made of solid oak. It weighed about the same as the sun, I think. I moved it for her when she moved into this place. After I'd come to her and asked her to help me get Liz back, she'd shown me how to set up the table for the ritual. I drew the pentagram with the chalk, like she'd shown me, making sure all the lines were not even, but shifted heavily to the left. Then I sprinkled the dust down the lines. She never told me what the dust was from, and I never thought to ask. Salt goes around the outer circle. I was nervous, so I used the whole box. I lit black candles and laid out Tess's Book of Blood at her seat. She had the ritual blade at the cutting block, quartering Max's heart.

Max had been my best friend. But I loved Liz more.

"All right," Tess said. "Let's begin."

She carried the quartered heart on a serving tray like it was a Thanksgiving turkey or the head of John of the Baptist, blood pooling darkly on the ornate, curved metal.

When I saw Tess's reflection in that blood, she was no longer beautiful. In the candlelight her features took on a darkness of malice and cruelty; she became twisted and grotesque, but only for a moment. She sat the gruesome sacrifice in the center of the pentagram and when she sat down behind the open Book of Blood, the light and shadows came together on her face to make her lovely once more.

"Sit," she bid me.

I sat in the chair opposite her, my eyes flickering in time with the flames, flashing from her face to the heart on the table and back again.

I remained silent while Tess worked. She took a mortar and pestle from a small wooden table in the corner and began to mix dried herbs. She checked the book before adding each new ingredient, flipping a page, running her finger down the text, as if this was not a dark summoning ritual at all. Tess could have been any girl at any library researching anything. But she wasn't. She was a witch. And in my grief, my need to have Liz back, I'd forgotten what that could mean.

Tess scratched a series of lines written in a language I'd never seen on a piece of paper and passed it over the table, over Max's severed heart, to me.

"I will begin the summoning," she said. "When I tell you to, you must read that exactly as it is written. You will need to sing it three times."

"I don't sing," I told her.

The Dismissal Song

"You do today."

"I don't know how to pronounce these words."

"Follow my lead," she said. "I will guide you."

As she began to read from the book the candlelight flickered. The hair on my arms and neck moved in a breeze that came from the center of the table. Then all those hairs stood up and froze in place as the temperature plummeted. It all happened so fast. Tess had barely spoken any words in that horrible, guttural tongue when something, some unseen force, pulled a quarter of the heart from the platter and onto the table, leaving a smeared trail of congealing blood dripping over the edge of the metal. I watched in terror as that quarter was consumed, bite by tiny bite, by an invisible entity at the center of the salt-laced pentagram. Blood clung to something in the center of the air and ran down an invisible chin. When that quarter of Max's heart had vanished, I could see the grisly outline of a blood-covered jaw. The candlelight flickered again and the creature in the pentagram became slightly visible. It was translucent, but the blood was giving it shape. Its eyes locked on mine. I could feel them boring into me. There was the shimmering shape of hair falling onto narrow shoulders. I couldn't be sure, but I felt, hoped, that this was Liz coming back to me.

Tess stopped chanting and told me to read the words she'd given to me.

I took my eyes from the ghost of Liz and read the first line silently.

"Now," Tess urged.

I began to speak, but she stopped me immediately.

"It's a song, Joe. These words must be sung by one she loves, and they must be sung correctly, with the correct inflections and rhythm."

"Maybe we should have rehearsed a bit," I said.

"No time now. Repeat after me. Exactly as I sing it."

As she led me through the eight lines of text, I could hear that the words were written with the rhythm and flow of poetry. That much was obvious, even if I didn't know the language. The words rolled up my throat and off my tongue with such easy grace I felt that this was not the first time I'd uttered them. It was a song begging to be sung.

The thing that was Liz sat motionless inside the protective barrier of salt until the song was finished. Then a fierce wind shrieked through the room, blowing out all but one of the candles. As Tess relit the other candles, I watched the ghost lift another quarter of the heart to its lips and bite into it. With each bite, it became more visible, presumably more tangible.

Again, Tess led me through the song.

Again, the wind came.

Again, the ghost consumed a quarter of the heart.

The thing before me had no flesh. It was a human being, flayed. There were muscle and veins and all the tissues that lie beneath the skin, but no skin. I was repulsed and entranced. This thing before me was the love I'd lost, that Max had taken from me, but it was hideous to look upon.

The Dismissal Song

It was Liz. Or almost Liz. I could tell by the eyes. She had appeared as a shimmering entity, a mirage. Then she'd taken on shape, substance. The third quarter had given her most of her humanity back, but much of her flesh was missing. The fourth quarter would bring her back to her former state.

Liz reached out her monstrous hand toward me, fingers splayed, her thin, flayed body leaning over the last quarter of the offered heart.

It was then that I noticed the salt had been disturbed. The wind had blown paths through the circle, spreading the little salt crystals all over. Between me and the thing I thought was Liz, there was no barrier.

Her hand broke the plane of the pentagram and the look in her eyes changed from pleading to hungry yearning. Both bloody hands on the table, the ghastly thing dragged itself toward me. I leaped from my seat, overturning my chair.

"The circle's broken," I screamed.

"Quick," Tess said. "Get the salt."

I ran to the kitchen counter and snatched the salt box, remembering only then that it was empty; I'd used the entire box making the circle.

From behind the skinless ghoul, other dark shapes were rising from the center of the pentagram. The thing that was Liz, and yet not Liz, dragged itself off the table's edge and lurched toward me. Its body jerked and twitched weirdly like a malfunctioning machine.

"What's happening?" I yelled.

"The ritual was upset," Tess said, her hands frantically, methodically, pushing the salt crystals together. She was trying to reconstruct the circle. "Quickly, give her the last quarter of the heart and sing the song again."

The song? I'd forgotten about the damn song. I glanced around, moving to keep distance between the thing I'd summoned and myself. I didn't see the paper anywhere. The room was all shadows and fear. Small, winged things were emerging above the table.

"What the hell are those?"

"Dark faeries," Tess said.

"You're shitting me."

"I told you that you were in over your head, Joe. But you insisted. You couldn't just let her stay dead. People die, I said. You have to let her go, I said. But you begged me."

"Well, what the hell do we do now?"

"You have to put her back in the circle so we can send her back."

"I don't want to send her back," I said. "She's here now. Let's just finish the ritual."

"It's been disturbed. We have to deal with the faeries. They must not escape."

Tess was pushing the salt back into the form of the circle, recreating the protective barrier.

"I'm not sending her back now that I have her again."

"That thing is not Liz. Not yet. It's just a ghast: the shape of her body with no soul. It needs flesh and blood—that's why we needed the heart of the one who killed her."

The Dismissal Song

"Max didn't kill her."

"What do you mean he didn't kill her? That was the point of choosing him."

"They were hit by a truck," I said.

"Max was driving when they had the accident."

"It was the other guy's fault, Tess. You said it had to be Max. You said Max by name. You made me kill my friend."

"I made you do nothing," she said. "You chose, Joe. You chose Liz over Max. His life for hers. It was always your choice. I tried to talk you out of it, but you wouldn't listen."

"You said it had to be Max."

"You led me to believe he was at fault, Joe. It doesn't matter now. Get that thing back into the circle and keep singing." She was outrageously calm just then.

"It doesn't matter?" I raged. "Doesn't matter? I killed him, Tess. I cut out Max's heart while he was alive."

"It was the only way," Tess said.

The dark faeries, long, black-skinned things that looked like shaved cats with bat wings, banged themselves against the ghostly wall produced by the frail, failing salt ring. They were repulsive creatures with mouths full of wicked fangs and little black pellets for eyes. Inside the broken circle, some of them were eating the last bits of Max's heart. Without that, there was no way to finish the ritual.

"You never mentioned faeries," I said. "What are we supposed to do with these?"

"There are many things I didn't mention," Tess said. Her voice was calm and commanding. She was in total control of the situation. "Devils, shades, vampires. There are thousands of things you know nothing of, Joe. You came to me because I understand these things. Because I have knowledge and power. Now do as I say, Joe. Get her back in the circle and sing the damned song."

Liz caught hold of my leg with both hands and bit in with a mouth full of inhuman teeth.

I howled and kicked. I kicked her so hard, she flopped onto her back, leaving blood and gore splattered on the floor and wall. I knew then that this was not Liz. This was something dark and evil summoned from the pits of hell. This was not the girl I loved.

Grabbing her by the legs, I dragged Liz to the edge of the table. Tess was leafing through that damned book, searching for the spell that would reverse this botched ritual and send these things back to wherever they had come from.

"Grab her arms," I said.

Together we hoisted Liz onto the table and shoved her toward the circle. At the edge of the circle, the salt stopped her from crossing over.

"Shit," Tess said. "We'll have to clear some salt away to get her inside."

Liz was struggling and flopping, trying to get to her belly. Thankfully, her legs appeared to not be working.

"Well, do it then," I said.

"We can't," Tess said. "We'll let the faeries out."

"To hell with the faeries," I said. "Let's get this over

with."

In a flurry of exasperation, I brushed away a swath of salt and began shoving the gruesome ghast into the circle. The salt along the lines was scattered as the thing flailed and thrashed. The faeries beat their wings furiously and a couple darted out of the circle the moment I disturbed the salt. I found myself punching the Liz-ghoul in the head, beating it back into the circle from which it was trying to flee. A faerie fluttered in my face, wings buffeting and its breath suffocating me. It raked my face with the talons at the end of its wicked bat-hands and bit deeply into my cheek. I tore at it with one hand while the Liz-ghoul bit into my other arm.

Tess was no help. The moment she'd let go of the creature's arm; she began thumbing through her book again. Now she had two escaped faeries to contend with. She screamed but I could not go to her. I had problems of my own.

I managed to tear the faerie from my face with my free hand and shove its face into some scattered salt. The thing hissed and screeched like a cat, buffeting and squirming under the weight of my hand. At the same time, I jerked my arm away from the Liz-ghoul, my wrist falling limp, my hand useless. She'd taken a hunk of the muscle out of the back of my forearm and without it I could not straighten my wrist.

With my good hand I scooped as much salt as I could back into position, trapping the ghoul and the remaining faeries in the circle.

Tess was still screaming. I turned to her. The two escaped faeries were on her, clawing into her face, chewing on her ears and nose. Tess's face was being torn to shreds. Soon she would look like the Liz-ghoul on the table.

There was pounding on the apartment door. Someone was shouting from beyond.

I rushed to Tess and pulled one of the impish creatures away from her. The creature came away with difficulty, bringing with it a long strip of her flesh caught in its mouth. A hole opened in Tess's neck, exposing the pulsing artery, and the other faerie latched onto it immediately, sucking the blood from her neck.

By the time I'd gotten the faerie I was holding back inside the circle, Tess was on the floor, dying.

The pounding continued at the door and this time I could hear someone yelling that the police were on their way.

The last faerie was in a frenzy, sucking the remaining blood from Tess's pale body. I grabbed it by the scruff of its neck and carried it with my remaining good hand to the circle. I managed to get everything back in place, the salt, the candles, and the summoned creatures.

Tess was trying to speak, but the blood oozing from her throat turned her words into senseless gurgles.

"What page?" I asked, picking up the black book from where it lay beside her.

She was weak, but she managed to hold up both hands

with fingers extended.

"23?" I asked her.

She nodded weakly.

The pages were numbered in Roman numerals, so at least I could understand that much. I found the page and held the book up so Tess could see it, but her eyes had glazed over. She was gone. She would be no help to me now.

Standing, facing the circle, I read the words from the page as best I could, pronouncing the jumbled words as phonetically as I could manage. This too, was a song. A dismissal song. I sang it as best as I could without music, rhythm, or someone leading me. The faeries hissed and flittered, trying to burst from the circle, mocking my song in screeching, rasping voices. The Liz-ghoul writhed, and her exposed muscles churned, dripping blood from her skinless body onto the tabletop. Darkness opened on the table, beneath the pentagram, and the faeries were pulled, one by one, down into it. I watched in horror as the muscles and tendons were stripped from the ghast's bones and it melted away into shadow. I finished reading the passage of the alien language. The dismissal song fell away, and the room went eerily quiet. A strong wind blew through the room, dispersing the salt and snuffing out the candles.

For a moment I was alone in total darkness and perfect silence.

The door to the hallway opened, spilling light over me, and over the mess of gore that had been Tess. Two policemen entered with the superintendent. They were shouting at me to put my hands up, so I did, still holding the book in my good hand. In the hall behind them, the building's residents had gathered.

Tess lay at my feet, face torn nearly off, throat opened, blood drained from her. I was covered in blood, some belonged to Tess, some to Liz. A bit was from the remnants of Max's heart, and I suppose some was mine.

I did kill Max. I admit that. I did a terrible thing for a good reason. But not Tess. The faeries did that. No one will believe me, I know. I'll spend the rest of my life here, in this place they call a hospital, talking to shrinks, swallowing the pills they give me, but none of that will change the truth.

I did what I did so I could be with Liz. But that wasn't Liz we brought back in that apartment, it was something foul and awful. The ritual could have worked; I believe that. But some things man was not meant to tamper with. Maybe we should leave the dead, dead. But I still feel that if I contact Tess, she could tell me how to make it work. She could tell me how to bring her and Liz and Max back. There's got to be a way.

~~~

Notes on The Dismissal Song

I had forgotten that this story existed. It was tucked away in the corners of my documents file on my computer, in a file labeled "writing projects from old laptop". It had a different title. One I did not recognize. So, one October night, while sipping a Moscow mule and listening to rain pour outside my window, I burned through the witching hour reading

The Dismissal Song

this old, unfamiliar tale.

Reading it, I enjoyed it, though it needed a little work. So, I touched it up and made it as good as it could be and gave it a new name and new life. I like to think that The Dismissal Song *has a hint of a Lovecraftian vibe, something maybe akin to* The Statement of Randolph Carter.

Someone Broke in and Washed My Dishes

A being is nothing other than what lingers.

Eliza Griswold
from *Ode to Thucydides*

Someone Broke in and Washed My Dishes

"Someone broke in last night."

We were standing on the little elevated patch of grey macadam concrete that passed for a front porch. The angles of the red- and brown-brick building casting eerie early morning shadows between us.

"Into your house?" My neighbor, Helen, lived in the adjoining brick townhouse. She stared at me, wide-eyed, shivering in the early spring air, pulling her pink bathrobe somehow tighter around her middle-aged frame.

"Yeah," I said.

"That's why the police were here?"

"They don't believe me; but I know someone was in there."

"How?"

"Come on in. I'll show you." I pulled open the white, aluminum-framed screen door and held it for Helen, gesturing for her to enter.

She just looked at me for a moment, a man in his mid-

Someone Broke in and Washed My Dishes

twenties inviting her into his home, and she wearing nothing but the pink robe stretched thin over her cold breasts. Helen hesitated, eyed me up and down, then reluctantly stepped up into my home.

"You've been in here before, Helen. Why so nervous? I won't bite."

She checked the half-bath just inside the door like a cop on TV checking his corners. I watched her step gingerly from the shoddy patchwork linoleum to the beige-brown carpet of the living room, her eyes taking in all corners, flashing to the narrow strip of kitchen on the right, to the hollow of the staircase behind the half-wall that sat behind my worn-down, torn-up old grey couch.

"It's not you, Ant," she said. Always I was Ant to her, never Tony, not once since I met her was it Anthony. From the beginning, we'd been friends. "It's just…a break-in. That scares me. How do you know they're still not here?"

I shrugged and walked into the kitchen. "I checked everywhere. Looked all over. No sign of anybody. Nothing but this."

Helen came into the kitchen, her wary eyes still taking in everything. She was observant. I knew she would see it before I pointed it out.

"Why would anybody do this?" she said.

"I don't know."

We were looking at the counter next to the sink. The junk drawer had been emptied. Everything was on the counter. Pens, scrap paper, twist ties, a flashlight, a box of

136

weather stripping and plastic sheeting from the winter, a cigarette lighter with a tiger on it. There was even a random domino—a seven, with two at one end and five at the other. The drawer was open and bare. Every last item was on the counter.

"Weird," Helen said.

"And this," I said, pointing to where my four Justice League juice glasses were lined up neatly on the other counter, next to the stove, near the peeling white refrigerator. The Flash, Superman, Batman, and Wonder Woman sat there, arranged perfectly, staring up at us. "I didn't leave those out. In fact, they were in the sink, dirty, when I went to bed."

"Why didn't the police believe you?"

"Nothing is missing. There's no *evidence.* All the doors are locked. No sign of forced entry. Hell, no sign of entry at all."

"What are you going to do?" she asked.

I poured myself a cup of coffee, which I'd set to brewing before the police arrived. They hadn't accepted any, but Helen did, and I poured her a cup, adding just a touch of French vanilla the way she likes it.

"What can I do?" I slipped into a chair at the little table that served for my breakfast nook and doubled for my dinner table. Helen joined me.

She sat across from me, sipping her brown brew, staring intently at my face as if searching for something. At last, she said, "Go up to Cabela's and get some security cameras."

Someone Broke in and Washed My Dishes

"I'll just get them on Amazon."

She reached out and grasped my hand, her eyes pleading. "You don't want to wait two days to install cameras, Ant. What if they come back?"

"You think they might?"

"I think they could. Just run up to the store, get some cameras—good ones, you know, like trail cams that activate by motion. Get them set up before tonight, and then we'll see what's what."

So, I did.

I spent a thousand dollars at Cabela's. I didn't have a thousand bucks to spare, but in the end, I had five cameras with night vision capability, which could record sound, were motion-activated, and would send the data to my laptop. By bedtime, there was a camera aimed at the rear sliding door, the front door, and the window in the kitchen. All points of entry. Plus, one outside my backdoor and one on the front porch, overlooking the steps and the parking lot, staring down at my Subaru, Helen's minivan, and her husband's pickup.

That should do. And not a moment too soon. It was nearly ten o'clock when all was done, and I'd wasted an entire Saturday. I was not yet twenty-five and should have had something to do on a weekend evening, but the whole ordeal had simply taken it out of me. When it was finished, I climbed the tattered carpet of the narrow stair and fell into bed, ready to sleep and put this whole thing behind me.

I set up my laptop and opened Netflix. Something funny

should help me relax. Watching an episode of "Living with Yourself," I finally dozed off with a smile on my face.

~

My alarm pierced the twilight like a distressed bird. Why did I have an alarm set for 7:30 on a Sunday? And why did it sound like that? Suddenly my head throbbed. I needed coffee. And I needed a new alarm.

I dragged myself out of bed and into the hall. There was a bathroom at the top of the stairs and another bedroom across the small landing. That door was always shut. I didn't use it for anything but storage, and my old writing desk was in there. But who needed the desk when I could do all my writing downstairs at the table? When I did write anything, that is. At that point, I hadn't even tried to write in a couple of years.

Moving out on my own, finishing college, working two jobs to be independent...well, all that put a real damper on my creative spirit.

On this morning, the door to my storage room/office space was open. Just a crack, mind you, but open, nonetheless.

I froze there, teetering between going downstairs to make coffee, popping into the bathroom to tend to early morning affairs, and tiptoeing across the tiny landing and pushing open that door, afraid of what I might find.

If a stranger were so inclined to break into my house for the second night in a row, what would draw them to that room?

Someone Broke in and Washed My Dishes

I stepped forward, apprehensive. Afraid to see what lay beyond, I set my fingertips against that hollow door and pushed it inward. The shades were open and the window on the far side of the room let in light from the parking lot. Nothing stirred in the shadows. There was no one there. Boldly now, I flipped the light on and went in.

My old writing desk, small and rectangular, sat beneath the window, top cleared off, waiting for me to come back to it and sit and write. Now was not the time. I looked closer. The desk was too clean. Where dust had settled onto other items in the room—shelves, books, boxes, my grandmother's old clock—the area in the center of the desk had been dusted off haphazardly, as if someone had simply dragged an arm across it. The chair was pushed in under the desk, as it had been.

Slowly, I moved toward the desk.

A sound from within the room startled me and I jumped. It was a loud click. No, a tick. A tick-tock followed by another. It wasn't possible. I turned to the clock—my grandmother's old clock that hadn't worked in twenty years. More. They say it stopped ticking the moment she died. But now it had started again, as I stood here, at my desk, staring at the dark mahogany box with the ring of brass surrounding the dark-numbered clock face. The time was frozen at 10:08. Whether a.m. or p.m., there was no indication. On either side of the clock face stood three small pillars of amber, each engraved with the swirling pattern of marble.

Forgetting the mystery of the desk, I walked slowly toward the newly functioning clock. There was no second hand, but the rhythmic ticking of each second sounded loudly in the room. Curious, frightened, I reached out for the clock. My fingers nearly upon it, I was stopped short as, from within the foot-long device, an alarm blared. A deep resonant ringing with the undertones and finality of a gong filled the room.

I leapt back, terrified. Then I fled the room and headed downstairs, the sound of the clock alarm fading away as I descended.

~

Somehow, things were worse downstairs.

The house was in disarray. Before I finished setting up the cameras the day before, I'd cleaned the kitchen, putting everything back where it belonged. What a wasted effort.

The chairs were drawn away from the table. One was in the kitchen, positioned as if someone had been standing on it to get to the cupboards above the refrigerator. Another was sitting next to the sliding door, as if someone had sat in it staring out at the thin veil of trees that passed for a 'forest' before running into the apartment complex next door. The third chair was still at the table, though it had been pulled out as if a person had been sitting there. In that spot at the table sat a notebook taken from the coffee table and a black ballpoint pen taken from the junk drawer.

The junk drawer was not emptied this time. Plates were stacked neatly on the counter, though, and a row of steak knives lined the sink basin. The bread was open, the twist tie lying beside the loaf on the counter near the stove. A pan on the stove, half full of water, was definitely out of place. I'd eaten out the previous day while shopping for cameras.

Cameras!

Suddenly I remembered them. I hadn't placed any upstairs, because what would have been the point? There was no entrance upstairs. Only windows that dropped straight off; no ledge on the outside to stand on. But still, I had five cameras pointing at the access points.

It was time to check the footage.

Swallowing my terror and bolstering my shaking legs, I made my way back to the base of the stairs. I felt like a small child, afraid of going into the basement or the attic. My dad would have something to say about this, I have no doubt. How could I be afraid to go upstairs in my own home? And what was I frightened of, anyway? A clock that had started ticking? An alarm? The ghostly removal of dust from a desk I hadn't sat at in a year?

Yes. I was scared. Of all those things.

I sprinted up the stairs, taking two, three at a time and, not even glancing at the storage room, I bolted into my bedroom, grabbed my laptop and charger, and leapt down the stairs, bursting out the front door.

Not knowing where to go, I found myself pounding on Helen's door.

"Did he come back?" Helen asked, standing there in her robe, steaming coffee cup in her hand. It was one of those novelty cups with a cutesy saying scrawled on it: *It's too early for this shit.* I could not have agreed more.

"Yes. Can I charge my laptop at your place and check the footage?"

"Hell yes," she said. "I can't wait to see this."

"Where's Dave?" I asked.

"Sleeping," Helen said. "Don't worry about him. He'll be out till noon. Now, dish. What happened this time?"

I told her everything as I plugged in the computer. About the clock, the desk, the door being open. I told her about the chairs and the kitchen. I did not mention my fear of the upstairs, but by the look Helen was giving me, I knew she'd guessed it right. She brought me a cup of coffee in another novelty mug. This one read: *I'm not sleeping, I'm just resting my mind.*

I read it twice, sipped the steaming black brew, and opened the camera footage application.

"Let's try the back door first," Helen suggested. "That seems most likely."

I agreed. If someone was getting in, that back door seemed the most likely spot. I clicked on the footage clip from the sliding door, outside, pointing off into the trees.

At 01:03:42 we got our first glimpse of movement. The camera had picked up something moving in the trees.

"Probably some high school kids from the apartment complex," Helen said. "God knows what they're doing out there at night."

But there weren't any shapes I could make out in the

trees, certainly not any high school kids. I couldn't make out anything in the bright green glow of the camera's night vision light. Everything seemed still.

"Right there," Helen said, pointing.

I followed her finger to the edge of the frame, and there I saw movement. Two fat shapes waddling through the underbrush at the edge of the trees. Raccoons. Big enough to set off the camera, but not clever enough to break into my place.

The next clip showed a stray cat.

The next, at 04:31:59, caught a bat flitting through the night. A cool image, but not helpful.

"Go back," Helen said. "About thirty seconds."

I complied, backing up the footage.

"There," she said. "See that?"

"A shadow," I said quietly. I would not have caught it if she hadn't pointed it out.

There was a shadow cast on the small square cement patio off the back of my sliding door. A shadow cast from inside the house.

I looked at Helen, and she looked at me. "Is there a camera that shows that door from inside?" she asked.

"Yes." I clicked over to the appropriate camera and began at the earliest clip.

There was nothing until 04:14:03. At that time, the camera came on because the lights in the living room came on. It was a single twenty-minute clip. I sighed deeply and pressed play.

A grey shadow passed over the beige carpet. There was a reflection in the sliding-glass door and something in the dark recesses of the black TV screen, but in the weird light of the night vision and the strange glare on the glass, I couldn't make out any features. But it was apparent from the images that there was a person in my townhouse.

There were some rustling sounds, muffled and distant. The noise of a chair being pulled away from the table and set down on the linoleum of the kitchen floor. Creaking and groaning as weight was applied to that chair.

We watched in awed silence for a full ten minutes. The clearest sounds in the room were Helen slurping her coffee and the dull thud of a pounding heart on the inside of my ears.

Someone had been in my house while I was sleeping.

Finally, Helen said, "Let's switch cameras. See what's happening in the kitchen."

Just as I was about to change frames and look at the other angles, the grey shadow began to creep into the edge of the frame, carrying another chair. I stayed my hand, waiting, watching. The figure in the frame moved into view, dining room chair grasped in its hands, and headed toward the back door.

"Is that…" Helen began.

"What the hell?" I said.

"It's you," Helen said. "That's you sitting at your own back door, staring out the window."

I paused the video and looked at Helen. "I don't think

that's me."

"Honey," Helen said. "That is most certainly you. Look, you're wearing the same clothes."

"Want to watch some more?" I asked, puzzled. I couldn't believe this was the answer. Sleepwalking? I've never sleepwalked. Never. And even if I had, how would that explain the clock? No. There must be more to this.

"Oh, yes," Helen said. "I'll make us some more coffee."

~

A full pot of coffee and an hour later, Helen and I had made it through all the videos.

There was no denying it. That was me, in every video, in each frame.

"Sleepwalking," Helen said, chuckling. "I don't believe it."

"Neither do I," I said, not laughing. This was somehow worse. Scarier. What the hell was happening?

"And here I was," she said, "scared to death that some nutcase was breaking into places."

"That's not me," I said again. "Can't be."

She laid a hand on mine and looked at me softly. "Give it some time to settle in, hon. That there, that *is* you, Ant."

It was too much. I'd read my share of science fiction— hell, I'd written some sci-fi back in the day—and I had seen my share of movies. This had some pod-people stuff written all over it.

Ghost.

Replicant.

Clone.

Doppelgänger. That was the word.

Somehow those possibilities were less terrifying than having no control over my own actions.

"You're thinking body snatchers, huh?" Helen said. "That's unlikely, you know."

"I know. But still…I just can't wrap my head around it."

"At least we know why the police didn't find anything."

"What about the clock?" I asked. "How do you explain that?"

"Maybe your subconscious is trying to tell you something, Ant. Why would you—*sleepwalking you*—go into that room, clean the dust off that desk, and set the alarm on that clock?"

"That clock doesn't have an alarm, Helen. That's the scary part."

"If I were you," she said, "I'd go back into that room and figure out what you were doing in there."

That was sound advice and I decided to follow it. I packed up my laptop and headed home.

Back in the spare room, I began by investigating the clock. To my relief, I found that there was an alarm setting on the back next to the winding key. Apparently, I'd figured out how to set the alarm. But why? What was I trying to tell myself? What was the purpose of my subconscious manifesting in order to scare me? Was that the goal? Was I trying to scare myself? If so, good job me. Mission accomplished.

Someone Broke in and Washed My Dishes

No. There must be something more. Something deeper. If I were awake, and in this room, what would I be doing? What message would I be trying to send myself? If I could just figure out what I would say to myself, maybe I could get a glimpse of what my subconscious wanted from me.

Exasperated, I went to my old writing desk, pulled out the chair, and plopped down heavily into the seat. With my elbows on the desktop and my head in my hands, I sat wallowing in thought. This didn't make any sense. This wasn't real life. It was like something out of a story I would have written, at this very desk, two years ago; back when there was time to write, and I wasn't submerged beneath waves of schoolwork and the burden of two jobs.

This whole situation was like something my writer brain would...

Wait a minute.

No.

Just...no way.

Suddenly, it fell into place. The pieces of this obscure puzzle began fitting together like the threads of plot tying up at the end of a bizarre story. Could it be?

I lifted my head from my hands, pushed back slowly from the blank slate that was my desktop. Slowly, I pulled open the center drawer.

There, in a small, neat pile, was a stack of lined papers. Words filled the spaces between the lines. Words written in a feverish flurry, scrawled with the energy of a tale burning to be told. Words written in a familiar hand.

A familiar story.

One I'd experienced recently. A tale still unfinished, waiting for an ending to be tacked on.

As I read through the words I'd written in my sleep, a message given to me by my other self, the one who needed to tell stories, the part of me that could not stand to not write stories, the message from myself finally broke through.

He was telling me to get back to work.

He was telling me to write something great.

I was telling me to air out this room, open my mind, and do the only thing that would keep me from going completely insane.

I was telling myself to write, that I *would* write, one way or another.

And if I wasn't going to do it, the other me would be doing it for me.

~~~

Notes on Someone Broke in and Washed My Dishes

This story first appeared on the competitive challenge writing website purplewallstories.com. *That site hosts many great stories each month that are pit against one another in a tournament that readers vote on. Go to* purplewallstories.com *and cast your vote daily for your favorite stories.*

People always ask where writers get their ideas. It's a trope as old as the stars. In most cases, I think I can answer that question. I was thinking of this, listening to this song, reading this book, or my friend said this, and it stuck with me. In the case of Someone Broke in

Someone Broke in and Washed My Dishes

and Washed my Dishes, *I don't have a definitive answer. I was struggling with some writer's block, which is crazy because I have so many stories percolating all the time that you would think I'd be able to find something to work on. In the midst of this writer's block, I began writing a story about a break in. I didn't know what it was about, who the characters were, or what was going to happen. All I knew was that someone had broken in and washed this guy's dishes. I, too, was surprised to find out why.*

The Weighted Blanket

And this maiden she lived with no other thought
Than to love and be loved by me.

Edgar Allan Poe
from *Annabelle Lee*

The Weighted Blanket

"You'll regret this," she said. It wasn't a threat, but a statement of fact.

Kirk knew she was right. Adrienne was the best thing that ever happened to him. She was the woman he wanted to marry someday, when he was ready; but her insistence upon marriage was driving him crazy. It wasn't that he didn't love her. He did. He loved her from the top of her pretty dark head to the soles of her size six feet. But love and need were different things, and the fact was, since Adrienne had given him the weighted blanket, Kirk felt that the comfort of the blanket was enough.

She'd surprised him with the weighted blanket one night when he was feeling down, saying, "It's a symbol of our life together." It was a handmade gift Adrienne had crafted by sewing a floral print comforter to a blue one with a layer of small marbles between. It was so comfortable, so relaxing, that Kirk was sure Adrienne had placed an enchantment on it. The blanket was absurdly heavy, but when Kirk lay beneath it all his troubles seemed to be pressed out of him.

All his troubles except one. Adrienne wanted to get

The Weighted Blanket

married. She wanted it to happen soon.

"We've been together three years," she said.

"I didn't say we couldn't get married," Kirk said, shifting beneath the weight of the blanket.

"But you've never asked."

"Neither have you."

"Do you even want to get married?" Adrienne asked. She was sitting on the edge of the bed, on top of the weighted blanket, facing away from Kirk.

"Eventually," he said. "Sure. I mean, we can if you want to."

Adrienne scoffed. "That's not very convincing."

"Do we have to do this now?"

"We don't have to do this ever." Adrienne went to the closet and began stuffing clothes into a bag.

"Don't go," Kirk droned.

"Why would I stay when you're pushing me away?"

"I'm not pushing you away."

"You're sure not pulling me close. You won't even let me sleep under that blanket with you."

"This blanket is my safe space. You know that."

"I know it, all right. I am supposed to be your safe space, Kirk. Don't you get that? And you should be mine. I'm sorry I ever made you that blanket."

"I like it."

"You love it," Adrienne said. "You love it more than you've ever loved me. I hope you're happy together. Hope it brings you all the comfort and peace you deserve."

"You're not really leaving, are you?" Kirk lay beneath the weighted blanket, eyelids growing heavy, slumber sneaking up on him. He was tired and he really didn't have any fight in him.

Adrienne slammed the lid of a suitcase and stormed toward the bedroom door. "You're not even going to try to stop me."

"Would it matter?" Kirk yawned.

"More than you know."

Kirk wasn't listening. Sleep was tugging at him. As if in a dream, he saw a vision of Adrienne hovering above his face, heard her speaking softly.

"You'll regret this," she said.

Then Kirk was sleeping, and Adrienne was gone.

~

Kirk was dreaming. He dreamed every night since receiving the weighted blanket. He took pills prescribed by Doctor Conklin, which helped him to rest and calmed his thoughts, but it was the security of the weighted blanket that provided Kirk with deep sleep and sweet dreams.

Tonight's dreams were dark, though, as Kirk felt the oppressive weight of something like a huge cat covering his face. He was being smothered. He couldn't breathe. Something immense was on his chest. He was being crushed!

Gasping, Kirk woke kicking beneath the weighted blanket. Its weight was anything but comforting now. He felt trapped, buried alive. He struggled to free his arms from

The Weighted Blanket

the constricting cover, at last bringing his hands out near his face. He pushed the blanket away. It was like moving a slab of pliable cement. Sweating, grunting, Kirk writhed his body free of the hefty cocoon.

He lay there panting, wheezing in the dark. The clock on the table read 11:47 p.m. He'd been sleeping only a few minutes. Adrienne may not have even left the apartment yet.

Kirk stumbled to his feet and went to the door. He searched everywhere. Adrienne was gone. He was alone, and his loneliness was crushing him already.

~

"What did you do then?" Dr. Conklin asked.

"I didn't do anything," Kirk said. He was tired. He hadn't slept in two days. "I just sat there on the couch all night, alone in the dark, feeling awful."

"Sad," she corrected. "It's important to name our feelings."

"Sad," Kirk said. "Lost. Lonely." He stared at the ceiling above the couch on which he lay. It was one of those drop ceilings riddled with tiny holes. His eyes had been locked on those holes for ten minutes. He was beginning to feel a kind of kinship with them. "I've been feeling all those things since Adrienne left. But it's the nightmares that are killing me. When I try to sleep, I feel like I'm caught in a vice."

"I think you miss her, Kirk, and that's okay. You had a long relationship with a woman you love and now it's ended."

"But I need to sleep."

"Are the meds helping?"

"Same as ever," Kirk said. He'd been in therapy and on sleep medication for some time, since long before Adrienne left. The only that had seemed to help him rest was the weighted blanket, but even now that seemed to help very little. "I don't think it's a medication issue. It's Adrienne. When I close my eyes, she's all I see. When I sleep, I have nightmares. It's like she's my only source of happiness."

"*You*," said Dr. Conklin, "are your only source of happiness."

"How do I get over her? How do I get her out of my mind?"

"You dated other women before Adrienne, didn't you?"

"Sure. A bunch."

"This may sound rash," said Dr. Conklin, "but maybe you should go on a date."

"It's only been two days," Kirk said.

"I'm not saying start a relationship or sleep with anybody, Kirk. I'm simply suggesting you go out and get your mind off Adrienne for a moment. If you believe all your happiness is wrapped up in this one person, maybe you need to experience some new people."

"I don't know," Kirk said.

"Well, I can increase your dosage, or prescribe something new; but I think the problem is deeper. In the meantime, go out with some friends, relax, try to get your mind off Adrienne for a night and see if that helps."

~

The Weighted Blanket

Kirk had only two choices: Josh or Lily. Josh was working that night, so Kirk called Lily. Kirk and Lily had dated off-and-on over the years and been close friends since the seventh grade. He hadn't seen her in more than three years, not since he began dating Adrienne, but if anyone could pull Kirk out of his downward spiral, it would be Lily.

Lily was a pretty blond with pale skin, a quick, fervent smile and the heart of a child. That night they walked the city streets, holding hands like they had in their teenage years, talking and joking, Lily's voice ringing like chimes, her eyes gleaming like candlelight in a mirror. She was refreshing. For the first time in a long while Kirk felt totally relaxed, completely secure in the presence of someone else. Normally only his weighted blanket could give him such relief from the stress and sadness of his daily life.

They walked along the boardwalk, out toward the water, where the never-ending carnival lights glistened against the dark sky and gently pulsing sea. He won her a teddy bear and she struck all the cups with the BB gun. It was like being fifteen again.

"This is great," Lily said, a Cheshire smile stretching her face, plumping her dimples. "I'm having so much fun."

"Me too," Kirk said. He bit off a chunk of pink and yellow cotton candy. "Thanks for coming out with me. It's been a rough couple of days."

"I get it," she said. "Breakups are hard. Well, not ours so much, but that's different."

"It is different," he agreed.

"We were friends before we dated; and we're still friends now." She smiled up at him and bit into a corndog-on-a-stick.

Kirk's phone pulsed in his pocket. He looked at the screen. It wasn't Adrienne, just a notification.

"You have somewhere to be?" Lily asked.

"Nope," he said, grinning awkwardly. "Just checking the time. It's getting late and I have to work tomorrow."

"We better get you home then."

Kirk shrugged. "I doubt I'll be able to sleep."

"Why's that?"

"Haven't slept much lately. Bad dreams."

"Nightmares?"

"Yeah, sometimes."

"I don't have anywhere to be in the morning," she said. "Maybe I'll hang out and see if I can help you relax."

Kirk's pulse quickened in his ears. The last time Lily had helped him relax they'd ended up in a passionate two-week affair that had nearly ruined their friendship for good. He didn't want to lose her too. In truth, he couldn't bear losing Adrienne and Lily in the same week. But he needed rest and couldn't seem to manage that on his own.

He stopped walking and looked down at Lily. She stared up at him with soft blue eyes, smiling coquettishly, her lips curved in that special way that said she was here, as she would always be here, silently promising to provide whatever Kirk needed from her. He didn't want to sleep with her tonight, nor did he think he should; but he didn't want to be alone. Loneliness brought on the nightmares.

"If you don't mind," he said, "I'd really like company tonight."

"I don't mind at all." Lily stood up on her tiptoes and kissed Kirk softly on his stubbly cheek.

~

He couldn't sleep again that night. Having Lily there beside him seemed to somehow make things worse. She had wanted sex, but Kirk hadn't. Whatever it was he was supposed to feel, it wasn't there, but had been replaced with overwhelming anxiety. He'd found it hard to breathe and had nearly hyperventilated, and so Lily, sweet, understanding Lily, had lain there in bed with him, coddling Kirk in her arms until at last he'd dozed off, briefly.

First, he'd dreamed of Adrienne. He dreamed he *was* Adrienne, somehow inside of her, feeling what she felt, seeing what she saw. She'd been there, on the boardwalk, and she'd watched him all night as he strolled with Lily, hand-in-hand, laughing like kids. In his dream, Kirk could feel the heat of Adrienne's wrath, the flames of jealousy, the sharp pain of betrayal. He could see her angry eyes boring into him, into Lily. He could hear the gentle undercurrent of some subtle words being breathed through the night: soft hissing he didn't comprehend, could not quite make out, but that he knew were spoken for him.

The dream that followed was black and cold. Kirk was alone in darkness, sucking in air that was too thick to breathe. His lungs burned. An intense pressure squeezed his ribs, pinned his arms and legs. He cried out for help, but the words caught, and he choked on them.

In the darkness, wind whispered, bringing with it words that he could not understand. The tone was sinister, foreboding, and the voice was undoubtedly Adrienne's. She was here with him in this dark place, but she was not here to help.

When Kirk's eyes shot open, he was staring into the darkness of the room. An elongated triangle of light shone on the ceiling from the streetlamps. Something scurried at the edge of his reason. He wriggled out from beneath the weighted blanket. The blanket seemed much heavier than it had earlier.

Lily must have covered him, he reasoned, then crawled under that weighted blanket beside him. The weight of the cover did not seem to bother Lily; it must simply be Kirk's weakened state that made it feel so heavy. Thankfully, he hadn't disturbed her with his nightmares or while struggling to climb out from beneath the heavy blanket. He watched for a moment, listening to her breathe, then he slipped from the room and left Lily to her rest.

~

He fell asleep on the couch and managed to sleep through the night until the sun came blazing in, spilling light onto his face. Blinking the sleep away, Kirk rose groggily and went into the kitchen. Once the coffee was brewing, he went to the bedroom to rouse Lily. It was nearly 7:30 and she would want to be on her way when Kirk left for work.

The Weighted Blanket

When he opened the bedroom door, Lily stirred. She sat bolt upright, pushing the heavy blanket from her, her face showing panic beneath its weight. Her eyes met Kirk's and went wide.

"You're up," he said. "I've got coffee on."

"Who are you?" Lily screamed, leaping from the bed and grabbing the closest thing to a weapon that was at hand: A candle in a glass jar. It was lavender field scent, Kirk's favorite. "How did I get here?"

Kirk held his hands up defensively and stepped forward. Lily cocked her throwing arm. "Not another step, asshole."

"Lily," Kirk said. "What the hell? We've known each other for fifteen years."

"I don't know you, creep. Move over there." She pointed to the far side of the bed. Kirk complied. Lily, arm still in a throwing position, headed for the bedroom door.

"This isn't funny," Kirk said.

"No shit," Lily called from the other room.

"Why are you messing with me?"

"Where the hell are my shoes?"

"You kicked them off by the front door."

"Forget it," she said. "I'm calling the cops."

"No," Kirk said, rushing toward the living room. "Don't do that." But Lily was in the hall, gone, and she'd taken Kirk's favorite candle with her.

~

"Lily was here?" Josh asked. He had shoulder-length brown curls that bounced when he talked. "What was she even

162

doing here this early? Nevermind. Don't care." He poured himself some coffee and leaned on the counter opposite Kirk.

"She doesn't know me, Josh. It was weird, man."

"She's known you longer than I have. You're telling me she got amnesia last night?"

"We went out and she came back with me. When she woke up, she flipped out, like I'm a stranger who abducted her."

"Hmm," Josh said. He sipped at his coffee and looked hard at Kirk. "Where's Adrienne?"

"She split a few days back."

"And you've got Lily on retainer already? That's kind of messed up."

"It's not like that," Kirk said. "I've got a serious problem, Josh. What if she really does call the cops?"

"I don't think it's an issue, Kirk. Everyone knows you two know each other. Hell, I can attest to that."

"But she acts like she doesn't know me, Josh. Like I'm a stranger."

"Everything will be fine," Josh said. "She won't call the police. I'll call her."

"What if she doesn't remember you either?"

"We're about to find out."

Josh thumbed his cell and held it to his ear. Kirk waited.

"Slow down," Josh was saying into the phone. "Have you called the police?" Josh shook his head and mouthed *She hasn't* to Kirk. "Well don't call them just yet. Because it's not what you think. Just trust me, okay? I have to ask you something. Do you remember Kirk Lloyd from school? No? Listen, this is going to sound strange, but you've known Kirk for years. Yes, really. Trust me, Lily. I know you're scared. Probably confused too. Get to a hospital and get checked out and call me after. I'll stop by later on, or tomorrow, but I really don't think it's a police situation." Josh hung up and looked at Kirk.

"Well?" Kirk asked.

"She doesn't know who you are." Josh drank his coffee and leaned with his elbows on the counter. "I told you not to date Adrienne."

"Don't start with that," Kirk said. "We've got a bigger issue right now."

"Adrienne might be the problem," Josh said. "You need to talk to Harlan."

"Who's Harlan?"

"Adrienne's old boyfriend," Josh said. "The whole reason I said to avoid her."

"Where does he live?" Kirk asked.

Eyeing Kirk up and down, taking in the rose-colored plush bathrobe and matching slippers, the circles under his eyes, and the quickly cooling cup of coffee in Kirk's hand, Josh said, "I'll have him come here."

~

Harlan arrived half an hour later. Josh let him in and led him to the kitchen where Kirk still sat at the counter, nursing his third cup of coffee. Harlan was a few years older than Kirk.

His eyes were circled with dark rings and his long hair was unkempt. He looked as if he'd had a few rough years that he hadn't quite gotten over.

"You're the new boyfriend, huh?" Harlan asked, eyeing Kirk. He extended a hand. "Poor bastard."

Feebly, Kirk shook Harlan's hand, wincing when Harlan pumped it firmly. "We've been dating a few years now, actually. Or, we had. She left a couple days ago." He rubbed his wrist and looked away.

"I can tell. Looks like you haven't slept much. Don't tell me: nightmares?"

Kirk nodded glumly. "Constantly. When I can actually sleep."

"You hearing a strange voice? A weird language?"

"In my dreams," Kirk said.

"I told him about Lily," Josh offered.

"Thanks," Kirk said. "You want some coffee, Harlan?"

"It's not just the dreams, though, is it?" Harlan said, taking a cup and filling it. He sipped at the coffee, grimaced. "This is weak." He scowled and set the cup down, pushing it toward Kirk. "Got anything stronger?"

"Beer in the fridge," Kirk said.

Harlan helped himself. "There's no beer in here, dude."

"Bottom shelf."

"Oh," Harlan said. "You mean these wine coolers. It'll have to do." Harlan set a six pack of flavored drinks on the counter, popped one open, and said, "You've heard this voice a couple times now, right? But you're so tired you can't tell if you're awake or sleeping or somewhere in between."

"Maybe," Kirk said, trying to remember when he'd first heard it.

"It's so," Harlan said. "Believe me. Once she curses you, you can't sort it out—the difference between reality and dreams, I mean. I've been sleepwalking for years."

Kirk's eyes were wide as the clock on the wall as he tried to make sense of what Harlan had said. "Did you say curse?"

"She cursed you," Harlan said. "Make no mistake. The girl's a witch in every sense of the word. Well, Romani, technically. Whatever. She can lay curses and lift them. Now show me what she left here."

"I don't think she left anything," Kirk said. "She didn't have much to begin with; she's a bit of a minimalist. She packed her bags and took all her clothes."

"Think," Josh prompted. "There's got to be something. Toothbrush? Hairbrush?"

"It would be something you would use, or touch, every day," Harlan said.

"There's the comforter Adrienne made for me," Kirk said. "It's a weighted blanket, very relaxing."

"I bet it is," Harlan said. "Probably puts you under quite deep. Did the other girl…" he looked at Josh.

"Lily," Josh supplied.

"Lily," Harlan continued. "Did she happen to come into contact with this weighted blanket?"

Kirk's eyebrows rose and his eyes went wide as he looked at Harlan. "She slept under it."

"I'd call that contact," Harlan said, grinning his approval, shooting Kirk with friendly finger guns and winking.

"It's not like that," Kirk said for the second time.

Harlan's smile faltered, then rallied itself. "Of course it's not. Show me this blanket."

In the bedroom the three of them stood at the foot of the bed staring down at the white, floral-patterned side of the comforter. It was rumpled and folded back on itself from when Lily had kicked herself free of it. The blue underside showed, revealing the thickness, the density, of the marbles that lay between the layers of materials.

"Looks like it weighs a ton," Josh said.

"It's gotten heavier since Adrienne left," Kirk said, staring blankly at the blanket, gripping his coffee cup like a trauma victim. "I thought it was sleep-deprivation that had made me weak; but if what you say is true—if she's cursed this thing—then maybe it really has put on weight."

"That's not what made you weak, dude," Harlan said, smirking, swigging his mango-flavored 'beer'.

"Why didn't Kirk forget Lily?" Josh asked. "Or himself."

"Adrienne is good at what she does," Harlan said. "She could set two curses on one object, one for men, another for women. Or maybe one specific to you, and another for anyone else who sleeps beneath this blanket. Either way, you say Lily lost her memory of you—of only you—and you haven't lost your memories."

The Weighted Blanket

"None that I know of," Kirk said.

"And we don't know if Lily had nightmares," Josh said. "She just woke up terrified and ran away."

"Are we in agreement," Harlan said," that this is the source of the problem, and we need to get rid of it?"

"Yes," Josh said.

Kirk hesitated. He didn't want to part with his blanket. Before Adrienne had left, this comforter had made him feel...well, comforted. He wanted that feeling back. "Is there no way to lift the curse and keep the blanket?"

"You can get another blanket," Josh said.

Kirk shrugged. "I really like this one."

"You have to get rid of it," Harlan said. "We have to burn it."

"If you're absolutely certain." Kirk sighed, setting his coffee on the dresser, and drifting toward the bed.

They each grabbed hold of the edges of the heavy cover and pulled.

"I don't think I can do it," Kirk moaned.

The blanket did not move. It didn't shift, or budge.

Harlan stopped pulling and stared at Kirk, wide-eyed, eyebrows arched. "So," he said, sniffing derisively, "you're *really* the new boyfriend, huh?"

"It's put on more weight," Kirk whined.

"Just pull harder," Josh said. "We're three grown men."

"Well," said Harlan. "Two of us are."

"We can lift a blanket," Josh said.

They heaved, backs arched, butts sticking out behind

them, feet planted, each man putting all his strength into pulling the blanket from the bed. The sounds of their grunting and heavy breathing were disturbed by a cracking sound, followed by a single, violent pop. Josh yelped, toppling forward, body stiff, and fell face first onto the bed.

"What is it?" Harlan asked.

"My back," Josh groaned.

"I heard it," Harlan said. He sighed and looked at Kirk. "We'll have to think of something else. Help me get him up on the bed."

"He's already on the bed."

"In a better position, I mean," Harlan said, rolling his eyes and shaking his head in exasperation, as if he'd had enough of Kirk after knowing him just fifteen minutes.

"I might need a doctor," Josh said.

"I'll get you some pain meds," Kirk said. "All I have is the nighttime stuff; it will make you drowsy."

"Whatever," Josh said. "Just give me something and let me lay here a few minutes."

They helped Josh onto the bed properly, placing his head on the pillows. His feet lay on the weighted blanket at weird inclines because the comforter was bunched up like the rock ridge at a volcano's mouth. He took the pills and lay back against the pillows, closing his eyes.

"Just let me rest a few minutes," he said.

"Come on," Harlan said, pulling Kirk by the arm. "Leave him be. We need to make a new plan."

In the living room Kirk flopped into an easy chair,

The Weighted Blanket

dejected, hunched over the cup of cold coffee as he rotated it thoughtlessly, staring into the creamy liquid. Harlan went to the kitchen and came back with the case of wine coolers. He took a seat on the couch and opened two of them.

"Wish you had some real beer," Harlan said.

"That's Adrienne's," Kirk said.

"No, it's not."

"I ran out," Kirk said, looking down into his coffee. "Adrienne left that here."

"No," Harlan's mouth twisted as he drank, "she didn't."

"Are you sure it's the blanket?" Kirk asked.

"You felt how heavy it is. Tell me that's not supernatural. Here," Harlan pushed a bottle into Kirk's lap. "You should have one of these."

"Just one?"

"That'll be enough for you," Harlan said.

Kirk twisted the cap off the bottle and sipped gingerly. He scowled and began gently shaking and swirling the contents.

"What are you doing?" Harlan asked.

"Trying to get rid of the fizz. It hurts my throat."

Harlan stared at Kirk, his mouth hanging slightly open as if he wanted to say something. He drained a bottle and went to work on another.

"So, what now?" Kirk asked.

"I'm out of ideas," Harlan said.

"How did you rid yourself of her curse?"

"I didn't," Harlan said. "Adrienne did something similar

to me, but it was a dreamcatcher. Four women reported me to the police over the course of two weeks. After Adrienne, I started having the nightmares, just like you. I figured it was psychosomatic, my brain telling me I missed her. So, I decided to start dating again, just to get my mind off her. But each time I brought a woman home, she'd wake up and not remember meeting me."

"But it's not a problem now?" Kirk asked. "How did you solve it?"

"I burned the dreamcatcher."

"That worked?"

"Those four women still don't remember meeting me. I was interviewed by the police a bunch of times. People look at me like I'm a creep. I wouldn't say it worked."

"That's not reassuring," Kirk said.

"The truth seldom is."

~

Harlan finished his fourth drink and standing, said, "I should check on Josh."

Kirk set his half-full, fully flat drink on the coffee table and followed Harlan. "Oh, no," he said, stepping into the bedroom. "That can't be good."

Josh lay there snoring, tangled in the weighted blanket that he had somehow slithered beneath in the few minutes he'd been sleeping.

"At least we can test a theory," Harlan said.

"What's that?"

"How does it affect men other than you?" Harlan went

The Weighted Blanket

to the side of the bed and rocked Josh's body. "Josh, buddy; it's me, Harlan. Wake up."

Josh stirred, his eyes opening, blinking wildly. "Harlan. I'm out of it. Whatever I took was strong." He tried to move and grimaced. When he sat up, his body moved slowly, stiffly, struggling against the weight of the blanket. "My back is killing me."

Kirk stood away from them, waiting for Josh to look at him, expecting the worst.

"Who's this?" Josh asked, tipping his head toward Kirk.

Kirk's heart sank. He'd lost both his oldest friends in one day. His phone chimed in his pocket, but it seemed unimportant. Everyone had forgotten him.

"He's an old friend," Harlan said. "Kirk. You don't remember him?"

Josh shook his head. "No. Sorry. Have we met?"

"Here," Harlan said. "Sit back down a minute. I have to talk to Kirk, then we'll get you to a doctor."

Kirk followed Harlan into the hall and closed the door behind them. "What the hell do I do now?"

"We could cut it into pieces," Harlan said, "and carry out little four-inch squares to the dumpster."

"There's no other way?"

"Call Adrienne," Harlan said. "Apologize for whatever you need to. Get her to come back. It's far too late for me. She's ruined me. But there is hope for you."

"Do you think she'll lift this curse?"

"No," Harlan said. "But if you give her what she wants,

I'm sure she'll let you keep your blankie."

"You really think so?"

Harlan didn't even look at Kirk this time. "I'm going to take Josh to a doctor. You're on your own now, champ."

~

"I've been waiting for you to call," Adrienne said. Her voice was soft as ever, relaxed, as if she didn't have a care in all the world. "What took so long?"

Kirk pressed the phone to his ear. He was sitting alone on his couch. "It just took me a couple of days to realize how much I miss you."

"Oh? Did you come to that conclusion on your own?"

"You helped a bit," Kirk said. "Will you come back?"

She came back that same day. Her bags were still packed, and she didn't say where she'd been. Kirk didn't ask. They stood in the entrance near the door, looking at each other. Kirk was conflicted, feeling love, admiration, fear, all directed at, or emanating from, this small, strong woman before him.

"Do you know what you've done?" Kirk asked.

"It can be undone, sweetheart." She smiled sweetly, flashing teeth. It was all a game to her.

"Will they remember me?"

"Everything will be fine," she said, "as long as we're together."

"And Harlan?"

"What of him?" There was venom in her tone. "He made his choice."

The Weighted Blanket

"I want Josh and Lily to remember me. Can you make that happen?"

"You haven't asked the right question," Adrienne whispered. She stood up on her toes and kissed him, looked deeply into his eyes, allowing Kirk to look into hers, to see what it was she wanted, what she had wanted for such a long time.

He understood then. It made sense. He knew what she wanted, and in a way, it was what he wanted too. It was what he had desired for some time though he hadn't really known it till now.

"Will you marry me?" he asked her.

"No ring?"

"I'll get you one. But I'm asking now. Will you be my wife, Adrienne? Forever?"

She smiled so brightly Kirk thought he might go blind. "Yes."

Adrienne took his hand and led him to the bedroom. They made love beneath the comforting weight of the heavy blanket and then lay together, her thin arms wrapped around him in that familiar way. He hadn't slept restfully in days and now found himself drifting into slumber. He was unafraid of sleep now. Adrienne was here and she would chase away the bad dreams.

~

Kirk woke to the sound of his cellphone humming next to his head. It could wait. He was content with the mesmerizing sound of Adrienne breathing softly into his ear.

Adrienne lay there next to him, the blanket pulled over the two of them like a shroud. She was awake, watching him, a satisfied smile and knowing look playing across her feminine features.

The phone buzzed again, then again.

"Answer it," Adrienne said.

"I don't need to," Kirk said.

"It could be important."

Reluctantly, Kirk looked at the phone screen. Josh was calling. Kirk put it to his ear. "Hey," he said. "What's up?"

Josh said, "You want to come out with us later? Me and Lily, and my old buddy Harlan?"

Kirk blinked and gazed over at Adrienne.

"Go ahead," she said, as if she'd heard what Josh had said. "If that's what you want to do."

"Sure," Kirk told Josh. "I'll meet you in an hour." He hung up and lay back, staring blankly at the ceiling. "They remember me." He sighed and started laughing. "Everything's the way it should be."

"Yes," Adrienne said. "Everything is just fine now. I told you it would be." She pulled the heavy blanket up over Kirk, tucking him safely in like a child. Then she laid her head on his chest.

They stayed like that for a long time, until their breathing synchronized, and their heartbeats melded together. It wouldn't be long now, Kirk knew, and the two of them would cease being individuals. They would be one unit, one

The Weighted Blanket

person, stitched securely together like two halves of a weighted blanket. The more he thought about it, and the longer they lay together, the more content he was to have Adrienne here, to have his friends back, to have his life back to normal. He felt safe, secure, satisfied.

Adrienne pulled Kirk close to her. "You are so special to me," she said. "It's good to be back in my safe space."

The clock on the stand moved, one hour, two hours slipped by, but Kirk didn't stir. His phone buzzed again, but the sound was drowned beneath Adrienne's enchanting words.

There was something dark in Adrienne's voice, something strangely familiar. Kirk was so sleepy, so comfortable beneath the weighted blanket, and too content in the arms of Adrienne to pay any heed to the subtle hissing beneath her sweet, spellbinding words. As he drifted off toward sleep, he was totally at peace. He had no regrets.

~~~

Notes on The Weighted Blanket

The story of the writing of The Weighted Blanket *is, in my opinion, as interesting as the tale itself.*

A press called Jolly Horror put out a call requesting horror stories that can make you laugh. I had never before tried to write anything with comedy in mind, so I took this project on as a challenge to myself. The Weighted Blanket *was the third attempt at a horror/comedy with this market in mind. The first two lay on my desk, unfinished but not forgotten.*

C. L. Phillips

The anthology was called Accursed. *All stories had to deal with a curse of some kind. A cursed object, specifically, if I'm remembering correctly. I began developing the characters for this story, the relationship between Kirk and Adrienne, before I knew what the curse was going to be. I didn't know what a weighted blanket was. Had never heard of such a thing. I was walking through Walmart one day, looking for towels, and came across an entire section of shelving dedicated to weighted blankets. I went home and began searching this term on the internet and learned that they are used for comfort.*

This story was also shortlisted, but not accepted in the end. I received the kindest email from the editor, who praised the story and said some immeasurably encouraging things to me. In the end, he said, he had room for just one more story in his anthology. It had come down to this one and another, and he liked that other just a tad more. He said, "it's a totally publishable story."

So, here it is, appearing in this collection for the first time.

A Candle in the Dark

I have been here before,
But when or how I cannot tell:
I know the grass beyond the door,
The sweet keen smell,
The sighing sound, the lights around the shore.

You have been mine before,—
How long ago I may not know:
But just when at that swallow's soar
Your neck turn'd so,
Some veil did fall,—I knew it all of yore.

Has this been thus before?
And shall not thus time's eddying flight
Still with our lives our love restore
In death's despite,
And day and night yield one delight once more?

Dante Gabriel Rossetti
Sudden Light

A Candle in the Dark

The Ship

The ship bobs and sways on rolling ocean waves. Wind howls. Starlight gleams on the water as cool sea spray splashes his face. He stands on the prow, hands gripping the rail, eyes watching the endless twilight horizon. This way lies home. Forward lies his love.

He longs for her. It has been too long since they've been together, ages since he's seen her face. She begged him not to go, said no good would come of it. Her begging turned to sorrow, her sorrow became rage. At last, when rage became despair, she bid him go, to follow his dark heart as it pulled him away from her for love of something greater.

—what was it?—

—what was greater than her love?—

"Nothing," he says to the wind. "Nothing was worth losing her."

—yet, you chased it—

—abandoned her for it—

—you haven't lost her—

A Candle in the Dark

—hehe. yes, he has—
—be kind—
—he's been gone too long—
—he's fallen too far—
—you're too cruel; leave him be—
"Leave me be."

He looks around the ocean, eyes straying from the horizon. All around he sees them, smells them, the rotting remains of the drowned, the slain. This return voyage was meant to be a time of rest, peace, relaxation. He should be rejoicing, for the evil is behind him; and ahead, home and love await. But there is no celebration, no elation. Instead, fear has come, doubt. The years of misery spent sailing this endless dark sea have taken their toll, driving the others to madness and death. He's alone in the dark, trying to ignore the decay about him, the corrosion within himself.

That same madness threatens to overtake him, but it will not. No, he will fight it. The darkness cannot take his mind while the soft light of stars prevails.

—it's coming—
—darkness always creeps in when you're not watching—

But he is watching, and the darkness is not complete. Stars poke small holes in the veil. A silver sliver of moon glows gently somewhere behind him. There is light in the dark, and the darkness wavers with each pulse of the black sea.

—the light will go out—
—it always goes—

182

—but it comes back—

—too late. it returns after twilight has done its work—

"Darkness has no place in me."

—darkness is you—

—you are darkness—

—there's light in him still. let the twilight do its work—

"There's a candle burning for me. She is waiting."

—where is the candle?—

—where is your light?—

"Somewhere in the distance." His eyes search the grey world around him, seeking a glimmer of hope. "There must be a light ahead."

The wind rises strong around him. Clouds shift, blotting out stars and moon. All the world is black now. All is silent. There is no sound from *them*. Water laps gently at the hull. He stares up into the sky, waiting for light to return, trembling in the cool breeze and cool salt spray.

The Beach

At last, he's reached the shores of his home. He steps off the ship, surveying the dim land. An aura radiates from nowhere, illumination from somewhere beyond the beyond. The darkness ebbs like the tide, brightening, then diminishing, leaving him in darkness, then revealing the vague world around him. Sand stretches left and right further than his vision reaches. Before him, a steep incline fades from sand into grassy land. Within him, turmoil swirls in a vortex of whispering voices.

—what is he doing?—

—why does he hesitate? does he know what must be done?—

—long journey ahead—

—darkness coming—

—you need light—

—make light!—

He shakes his head, clearing away the noise within. He hates *them*, yet he needs *them*. *They* will guide him through the shadows until he can see the light from home. The candle she burns for him will bring him in, return him to her; first he must navigate the gloom. For that he will need to heed *them*.

"Show me the way."

—give me light!—

The ship carries nothing now but sorrow, misery, and the dead: the remnants of his wanton life. Nothing has survived the voyage to this shore. He is alone once more, longing for her touch.

—she won't touch you—

—no. she won't have you—

The land before him is darkening, fading to black. He needs the sea no more, so he burns the ship and heads inland.

—she won't be glad to see you—

—leave him be—

—you've gone too far this time—

—been gone too long—

"Shut up," he says. "All of you."

—you flee—

—into blackness—

—you'll be all right; we are with you—

"Leave me be," he says again. He shakes his head to empty his mind, but still——

—he's leaving the fire behind—

—leaving the light—

—no, no. go back—

—you mustn't leave the light—

—he must stay in the light—

—if he dies, we die—

—all of us—

"I won't die. The danger is behind me; I've left it beyond the sea." The light from the burning ship is far behind him now. He's off the beach and on hard ground. Before him stands endless black that no light pierces. Above him, full dark, no stars. There had once been a moon, hadn't there? Where has it gone?

—why is he looking up?—

—looking for stars—

—seeking the moon—

—haha…they're all gone—

"They will return." A cool mist settles on his brow, stealing the heat from the burning ship.

—no moon, no light—

—you're alone in the dark—

—not alone. never alone. he's got us—

A Candle in the Dark

—we aren't real—

In total darkness now, in endless silence, he steps slowly, treads softly, hands stretched out before him, eyes wide as an owl's as he seeks light. There is nothing. No sound. No scent. No breeze. Yet there is cold settling into him. A penetrating freeze, thick as the murk pressing in on him, sets his hair on rigid edge, rattles his bones.

Shivering blindly, he presses on. Home is inland. He must press on, put distance between himself and the shore.

His teeth clatter in his ear, competing with the sounds of *them*. He tries to drown *them* out, focusing on memories of her. She is ahead, beyond the dark, and there in the dark she has left a candle burning as she promised she would. Each time he takes a voyage, she burns a light to guide him home. He has been lost before, but with her help he has always found his way back. He needs only to push on now, search for the small flame in the distance and, once he glimpses it—he needs only one glimpse—to head toward it.

—not this time—

—no candle—

—she promised. she does not break promises—

—he does—

—he's gone too far this time—

—no redeeming him—

—there is always redemption—

—always forgiveness—

—not for the truly lost—

—redemption is for the lost—

There is a sound in the dark. Something heavy thump-thump-thumping not far behind. He whirls about, trembling hands raised. He sees nothing. Only emptiness. Still, in the distance, faint—thump-thump-thump—three rhythmic beats like a devil knocking at the door.

—they're catching up—
—they always do—
—turn around—
—keep moving—
—they're coming for you!—

Spinning desperately, he readies himself to fight, to contest the darkness. Memories of her slip away, tumbling from his thoughts, frantic fear replacing them. Something is here in the blackness. It's near, and it's getting closer. Thump-thump-thump. Softly but steadily it moves closer, coming up from the beach, from the sea, from somewhere he thinks he's left it behind. But it will not be lost, it won't be shaken. It will hound him, haunt him, stalk his steps. Oh, yes, he knows what it is now, knows what each of the three sounds were—thump-THUMP-thuuummmp—the same, but different. Connected, related, but each standing alone to bring its own threat.

Forward now. Steadily and swiftly, he continues moving. "Guide me," he says. "If you're going to speak, then help me."

—closer now—
—watch out—

A Candle in the Dark

The Forest

He smashes into the tree, scraping his arm and face against the branches and stiff needles. There's a tightness against his forehead, squeezing at his wrists and legs. It is fear. He pushes it away, tries to squirm free, but the pressure endures, so he submits. He can bear the pressure, the oppression of the darkness, as long as his feet carry him home.

The scent of pine, of earth and flowers, floods his nose. He's reached the forest. Home is far away, but he is moving in the right direction.

The trees assault his body as he pushes forward. Growls, faint and far away, flutter on the chilled air to fall on his lonely ears. It is the only sound that is not him: the growls and constant muffled thump.

—*they are here*—
—*all around*—
—*press forward*—
—*relent*—
"I won't."
—*just give in*—
"No."

He moves slowly through the darkness, following just one voice: the one that tells him to move forward, to press on. The others are liars. Aren't they?

Around him, in the darkness, shades of deeper black limned with soft coronas. They are men, or men-shaped,

188

and they are near him, following him through the trees.

"Who are you?"

—they won't answer—

—they are from elsewhere—

—from beyond the darkness—

"Take me home."

—we are—

—you won't make it—

—keep moving forward—

—you're not ready—

—look for the light—

—you'll die in this forest—

He shuffles slowly forward, gently placing one foot before the other, hands reaching before him. The auras from the shadow-men illuminate nothing, only bring light to his fear. The further he peers into the darkness, the more he struggles to see. The shadow-things are there, then they are gone.

He blinks, looks again, unsure he's seen anything at all. Is his mind deceiving him? It could be *them.*

—it isn't us—

—we're here with you—

—they are outside—

—from beyond the veil—

He won't allow *them,* or the shadows, to hinder him. Somewhere in the distance, a fire burns on a hearth. He's too far away to feel it, but he aches for its warmth.

The pressure on his arms and legs intensifies, as if he's

caught in a vice. The pressure on his brow holds steady, neither increasing nor receding.

—steady now—
—almost there—
—there is a clearing ahead—
—watch out—

Sudden pain jabs his head as the pressure becomes a push, a thrust. Something has struck him with force: something deeper than a physical blow. Before him, a shadow rimmed in light looms, bearing down on him. He closes his eyes, recoils, finds himself rooted in place.

Then the shadow is gone. The pain in his head recedes, sitting like a burden, but weighing little.

The Clearing

Suddenly he is out of the forest. He can sense it, open space before him. Clear air, the scent of sweet flowers. The shifting of the ground, the strength of the wind on his face. He's reached the clearing beyond the woods and his home is near.

Across the expanse, a single light shines in the night. Dancing, flickering, the small pale pillar calls to him, beckoning him toward home.

"I'm coming," he whispers.

He can feel the weight of his absence now, the lingering feeling of exile. It's as if he hadn't left by choice after all, but had been driven away, sent to a far-off land to do battle with an unknown enemy in a world he can't quite recall.

That is home glowing warmly in the night, he's sure of it. Yet it seems strange. He feels he's a stranger now, returning to a foreign land. She would be there, waiting for him, but would she be the same? Would he?

He'd like to ask *them*, but *they* have gone. When the shadow vanished, taking with it the strange illumination that had surrounded him, *they* disappeared as well. Or, at least, *they* have fallen silent.

His eyes are fixed on that distant light. It's all he needs now to guide him through the empty silence.

The journey has been long. He's tired and cold. The night is dark and lonesome. But even from here he feels her warmth, her love, her grace. Soon now. Soon, he'll be with her.

Ahead, the light goes out and the world goes black once more.

His feet stop. The twisting pressure on his arms and legs subsides. His limbs feel light as feathers. His entire body is light, free of all bonds. He searches the sky, the world around him, seeking a light, a guide in the night; but there is nothing. He is alone with silence.

Suddenly, he wants *them* back.

"Help me," he whispers, praying *they* will guide him.

No answer. *They* are gone.

Hesitantly, he steps forward, pushing onward without prompting, without guidance, trusting that the light will return. The world is quiet. The wind is gone. He is in a land of stillness. Only his feet move in this place, treading lightly, heading home.

The Candle

In the void of darkness, the feeling of exile returns. Has he been abandoned now by everyone? Have *they* fled from him? Has she sensed him coming and snuffed the light, seeking to trick him, to trap him in the darkness? No, she would not abandon him. Still, he is alone now, frightened.

He dares not turn left or right but works to keep his feet aimed in the direction they had been when the light went out. But how can he know if he is facing the right way? Has he veered? Has he somehow strayed from the path? These questions seem to come from deep within, yet from something external also, something far away and long ago.

There had been a path, hadn't there? A straight path he'd meant to follow. Then *they* had come, whispering, laughing, mocking, sometimes mingling truth with lies and pulling him from the path. He had harkened to *them* though, hadn't he? Time and again, he'd believed what *they* told him.

Their words had confused him, turned him around, taken him far away from her. Now *they* are gone, and she is near, but without *them* he fears he cannot return to her. He doesn't know the way.

His legs stop moving. They are suddenly heavy. His body feels weary. He stands there once more in the darkness, looking this way and that. And here in the clearing, so close to her, despair steals his heart away, like so many things have stolen it before. He puts his head in his hands, covering his face and aching eyes, and he weeps.

In the distance, a small creaking sound echoes in the night. It's like wind whispering through a keyhole, bidding him lift his weary eyes to spy some hidden truth. He lifts his eyes to the vast gloom, and he sees the salvation his heart longs for. There before him, sitting on the far, dark horizon, is a small flame, flickering in the distance.

Abandoning all caution, he lurches forward, shuffling, stumbling, his legs not cooperating; and yet he breaks into a sprint, closing the distance between him and that single spark of hope. His eyes never leave that dancing flame but drink it in as he draws nearer.

At last, his long journey is coming to its end. His feet leave the soft earth he has been treading upon as he steps onto a hard, unyielding surface.

The surface is cold, and he realizes for the first time that his feet are bare. His legs are bare to the knee.

The wind kicks up once more as he reaches the small flickering flame and passes through the thin white garment that swaddles his otherwise naked form. His legs are tired, his arms weak. The pain in his head throbs as he steps toward the light.

The flame goes out and all is lost to the dark yet again.

Despair squeezes his heart. Something hard and dry clumps in his throat.

Before him, a door opens. Pure white light blinds him,

sends waves of anguish through his head. He shuts his eyes tight and staggers forward, listing like a lost ship, falling into the arms of the one he's been seeking.

She holds him close, pulls him upright.

For a moment, there is only him and only her. For a moment, there are only her eyes peering deep into his. For a moment, he is known completely, as he knows her, as he's always known her.

There, in her arms, he weeps once more, all despair flowing from him as he's overcome with joy. Her grace swaddles him. Warmth surges through him, a deep affection coupled with a wholesome heat. It is what he's yearned for.

"I'm sorry," he says. "So sorry. I didn't mean to hurt you. It won't happen again; I swear."

"Yes, it will," she says. Her voice is velvet, her touch silk. Delicately, she says, "Let's get you into bed. Everything will be all right in the morning."

He holds to her, clinging like a weakened child, as she leads him by the hand and helps him into bed.

Her eyes are like stars. The crescent pendant she wears glimmers like the moon. About him, the bed shifts like rolling waves, then settles to a calm as he stills. She releases him, and stares down with that sweet, radiant smile that lights up the gloom of the small sterile room.

"You're so good," he says. "I won't go again. I love you."

"I know," she says. "I know. Get some rest." She touches his head with a cool, soothing hand.

"Could you leave a light on?" he asks. "I don't like the

dark."

"Of course, I will. Goodnight. I'll be right outside when you wake."

When she's gone, the darkness returns, pressing in about him, smothering him. But it doesn't take hold for long. Soon, a small flame flickers in the distance, and he is at peace.

He's made it back to her, and the candle is burning for him just as she always said it would.

~~~

Notes on A Candle in the Dark

A Candle in the Dark *was written for an anthology called* Nox Pareidolia *that was released from Nightscape Press in 2019 but was ultimately not chosen for that collection. It was shortlisted for publication in that book, and I received a very kind email from the editor saying he would like to hold on to this story for a second volume. Well, COVID-19 came along, and I don't think that other volume ever came into being.*

The call put out from Nightscape Press for this anthology asked for "ambiguous stories in the vein of Robert Aickman." I hadn't read anything by Aickman at that point, so I started combing through some of his short stories, getting a feel for his style. Then I found it, tucked away in Masterpieces of Terror and the Supernatural, *a book that had haunted my shelves for years.* The Hospice. *This classic tale from Robert Aickman had an incredibly ambiguous ending and set the tone for a new train of thought in my mind.*

Meanwhile, I had been listening to a couple of my favorite songs on repeat. Home Again *by Chris Rice and* Inland *by Jars of clay (my favorite artist and favorite band respectively). Reading* The Hospice, *along with some Poe and Lovecraft, coupled with these two songs, gave birth to a type of story I had never attempted to write before.*

Fireflies

Don't wait. The time will never be just right.

—Napoleon Hill

Courage isn't a brilliant dash,
A daring deed in a moment's flash;
It isn't an instantaneous thing
Born of despair with a sudden spring
It isn't a creature of flickered hope
Or the final tug at a slipping rope;
But it's something deep in the soul of man
That is working always to serve some plan.

Edgar Albert Guest
from *Courage*

Примечания

Fireflies

Just before I dozed off last night, I had a vision. My bedroom filled up with fireflies. Hundreds of them. Little sparks in the darkness like Morse Code or primitive binary. As my eyes drooped, the fireflies began congregating on the ceiling just above me. I think they were trying to communicate.

It would have been nice to stay awake and see what happened, but I hadn't slept in a week and just couldn't keep my eyes open any longer. You see, there's this girl. There's always a girl, right? Well, this one is elusive and challenging. The type that sends you signals. That should be great. Sounds great. But in this case, half the signals say I'm into you and all the rest say Nope.

Maybe you know such a lady. Mine can't be the only one.

So, like any thick-skulled man with signal-reading-deficit-syndrome, I can't sleep. The moment my head hits the pillow, my mind is a fucking chatterbox. Scroll through every line of dialogue. What did that mean? Why did I say that? When she laughed, was I funny or was it fake? Good

Fireflies

fake or bad fake? And what the hell did that text message she sent me mean?

Seriously, it's been weeks of this. I really only sleep after I've been insane for three straight days.

Which leads us back to the fireflies. Were they real, or was it my sleep-deprived brain? I couldn't rightly say, so I skipped out early from work and went home. A cursory glance at the bedroom showed that fireflies had infested cockroach-style. They were on the desk in the corner, on the walls, on the curtains, on the bed. It was daylight outside, so they were sleeping, all piled together like ladybugs, fiery little behinds dark and cold.

First instinct is, of course, to get rid of them. I mean, an infestation of any sort of insect seems, to me, like a bad thing. But I could not shake the idea that they had been trying to tell me something. For some reason, a horde of lightning bugs had swarmed into my chamber, swirled around like glitter in a glass, then came together before my eyes in a kind of harmony, or at least a pattern.

So, I closed the bedroom door and left the critters to their rest. I needed them at peak performance at bedtime.

Now I was faced with the problem of how to spend the rest of my day. The only thing that had managed to keep this girl, Nicole, out of my head was my work. Shitty part? You guessed it. She works at my office. So while I'm at work, distracting myself from her with work, she is there distracting me from work with herself. And now that I'm home with half a day off, what else would I do but pine over her, waste the day thinking about how to win her over, wondering if she likes me, and stalking all her social media sites? You're probably thinking how there is just so much I could be doing with my time. Reading. Writing a story. Starting the novel, finally. Gardening. Jogging. Volunteering. Listen, man, whatever it is you think would be a better use of my time, I've thought of it too.

But infatuation is an unwieldy, evil bitch. She's right there in your ear, nagging. Constantly. Infatuation is like a jealous girlfriend who's trying to keep all your attention focused on this one girl. If you know, you know. Can't sleep. Can't eat. Suddenly lose a bunch of weight and everybody is like Wow! You look great! And you smile and thank them and inside you're all like FUCK YOU. Everything hurts and I'm dying.

But, hell, I'm no drama queen, so I take the compliment and go starve myself.

The other thing romantic fixation does is push your mind all the way to the edge of every extreme. You find yourself praying at night, calling out to the darkness for this thing to happen. You seek God. You beg the universe. You search for meditation and dating coaches and love life advice. You ask all your buddies, and you try to explain what the interactions with this woman are like and you've got shit so skewed in your brain that all your friends say the same thing: "Yeah, dude. This chick is definitely into you." Which, of course, is very encouraging. But then you go and talk to her, and her feet are pointed to the door and her eyes are glued to her phone. That can't be good.

Next moment, though, she's smiling and laughing and telling you you're the best. Saying shit like, "You're great." What she really means, I think, is, "You're great for someone else!"

So, fuck it. What harm can it do to wait to see what some invasive fireflies might have to say about the whole affair?

I spend the rest of the day kicking around the house with nothing to do. Oh, I could go the gym, or call a friend, or run down to the library. Hell, I could even finish that novel I started reading three months ago—back before I met Nicole. But instead, I bounce a ball against a wall and play out scenarios in my head.

My favorite is the one where I take her aside, leading her by the elbow like a player, and look deep into her eyes like we've been in love for a million years. In this fantasy, I say, "Look. I like you. And I think you like me too. I want to take you out Friday night. Text me your address and I'll pick you up at six."

In this fantasy, she leans in close so her beautiful brunette curls tickled my face, breathes softly into my ear, and says, "It's about fucking time, cowboy."

There are others, but I like that one best.

The day is spent just like that. Throwing the ball against the same wall over and over until a hole wears through. Then I switch walls. I toss the ball and I deliberate with myself. Should I just ask her out already, or not? And the other question: what the fuck am I so scared of? Rejection?

Hell no. I'm a writer. Rejection comes with the territory. Toughen up, Buttercup, or stop submitting your work.

What I'm afraid of is acceptance. Absurd? Yep. But there it is, I think. If she is into me, what the hell am I going to do with that info?

First off, I guess I could finally get some sleep.

For the remainder of the day, I think of all the conversations I've had with Nicole. All the times we've joked about dating sites and dating coaches and how some men are just hopeless. Men are the worst at picking up signals, she says. No shit. The signals are veiled and they're always so mixed. We talk about what works and what doesn't. We talk about everything. Everything. It's like we're best friends, which leads me to that dreaded phrase: Friend Zone.

Which leads me immediately to despair. I think I've really fucked this up.

Now what do I do with that? If we're friends, and I go for more, does that crush our friendship? Do I lose her all together? If I ask her, what are the options?

1. She accepts. Everybody's happy.
2. She declines. We remain friends.
3. She accepts and it ends horribly. I lose her all together. Forever. We are no longer friends.
4. She declines. I cannot handle it and I get angry/bitter/sad/depressed/aggressive/mean etc. We are no longer friends.

Fireflies

It's Pascal's Wager. That's what that is. But what does he know? Pascal's postulations on whether or not to believe in God seem simple when weighed against matters of the heart. Look, whether creation or evolution, somebody explain to me the use for heartache, anxiety, and self-doubt. I don't have a use for any of it, yet I can't drop any of it. I need an answer. Something concrete.

So, finally, when the sun's long gone and the night wears on, I make my way into the bedroom, alone.

Now I lay me down to sleep. But I know better. No sleep will come. Just me staring into darkness, thinking of her, wondering if she's thinking of me.

But the darkness is brighter than usual tonight. Tonight, the flickering tails of a thousand fireflies light up my bedroom. For a long time, I lay still and watch them buzz by and frolic. Some land on the walls and other surfaces. Many land on me. I feel like a Christmas tree with strands of light blinking and winking on all my limbs.

Their presence is calming, relaxing. Soon, I find myself dozing once more, being lulled to sleep by the soothing lights. Still, I'm sure they are trying to tell me something. But it's no use, my eyelids are too heavy. Darkness takes me the way the moon takes the night.

Sometime later, I wake. This will surprise you, I'm sure, but I'd been dreaming of Nicole and now that I was awake, she was the first and only thought in my mind. The second thought, of course, was, what should I do?

The easy answer is: stop being a pussy.

The fireflies seemed to agree.

Above me, on the white ceiling, the entire swarm had come together to spell out three words in big, illuminated block letters. The universe—and the lighting bugs—had finally sent me a sign. That sign said:

JUST ASK HER

"Okay," I mumble. Then I'm asleep again.

~

Next morning they're gone. All of them. Not a single firefly anywhere in the house.

~

At work, Nicole meets me at the copy machine.

"Feeling better?"

"A bit," I say. "Just going through some stuff."

"What kind of stuff?"

I smile at her and it feels weak, forced. My eye contact sucks. Can't bring myself to look at those lovely blues for two full seconds. "Girl stuff," I murmur.

"Oooh," she coos, touching my wrist. "Can I help?"

"More than you know," I say, not quite meeting her gaze. "I'm trying to win my dream girl. I need all the help I can get."

She smiles and leans in close. "I don't think you need any help. You're doing great."

"Am I?" I stand there looking down at her, enjoying the moment. Her hand on my arm is just the thing I've been yearning for. "What I'm doing doesn't seem to be working."

"It's working for me," she says. "But now you have to

tell me. Who's this dream girl."

I look into her eyes, briefly, and I'm flabbergasted. Then I say, "Sometimes I feel like you're not even paying attention."

It was hard to keep my eyes on hers for all the embarrassment and discomfort I was feeling. I felt myself begin to fidget and now my eyes were darting around the office, seeing everything except what was right before my eyes. When I finally turned back to her, Nicole was staring at me, the beginnings of a coquettish smile spreading slowly across her face. There was light in her eyes, a sudden flicker, as if those beautiful blue orbs were trying to tell me something.

I thought of the fireflies, and of the message they had so carefully spelled out for me. Just ask her, they had said. Well, what the hell? Why not?

My gaze met hers. The flutter in my stomach subsided and for an instant all my nerves were steel. "It's you," I said, surprised by my own boldness. "It's always been you. Would you like to have a drink with me?"

"I thought you would never ask," she said, her smile deepening, her eyes twinkling with something akin to delight.

"Tonight?" I asked. "After work?"

"Yes," said Nicole. "I know the perfect spot."

"Yeah?"

"A little hole in the wall downtown," she said. "A place called Fireflies. I think you'll like it there."

C. L. Phillips

~ ~ ~

Notes on Fireflies

I work nights. Long nights. Twelve hour shifts through the dark tide when most of the world sleeps. This makes my sleep schedule erratic. Sometimes I end up sleeping in strange places. One afternoon in early spring, when the snow began melting and the insects came out of hiding, I had fallen asleep in my recliner, in the living room, in the middle of a sunny day. I did not have to work that day. There was no alarm set. I simply slept until I was finished sleeping.

When I woke, dusk had come and gone, and twilight was fading fast. I was alone in the house but for a multitude of fireflies lighting up the ceiling above me. There were so many. Perhaps a hundred. It was eerie and kind of exciting. They moved around the ceiling, tails alight and flickering. None of them flew. The just stayed there, affixed to the ceiling above me. In my groggy, semi-awake state, I thought, "What are they trying to tell me?"

I went back to sleep for a while and when I woke up, most of the fireflies were gone, but the questions remained. Were they trying to communicate with me? If so, what were they telling me?

Poorly Executed

When the wind works against us in the dark,
And pelts with snow
The lower chamber window on the east,
And whispers with a sort of stifled bark,
The beast,
'Come out! Come out!'--
It costs no inward struggle not to go...

Robert Frost
from *Storm Fear*

Poorly Executed

<u>Part 1: The Pyre</u>

The townspeople came early to the burning.

Within the wooden palisades, the cramped town square was crowded with onlookers. Captain Louis Littlewood stood before the cold pyre, breathing in the crisp morning air, not looking at the fifty residents of this hamlet, but staring off over the distant trees, watching the eastern horizon. He was waiting on the sun. It was best to burn a witch at dawn.

This witch, for her part, was watching Littlewood, and had made no sound since Littlewood's men had bound her to the wooden pillar at the pyre's center. She simply stood, slumped ever so slightly in her soiled white gown, red hair hanging in matted clumps, streaked and caked with blood, sweat and mud, calculating blue eyes boring defiantly into the captain's. She had put up a fight when Littlewood's men had come for her. There was no fighting now. No strength left in her that Littlewood could see. Her hands were bound to the stake, above her head. Her torso was stretched vertically like a cat sunning itself. She was a pathetic sight, slouching and utterly helpless. Littlewood's men had not been gentle with her.

Dobbs and McCutcheon were violent, headstrong men. Not the types Littlewood would have chosen for his company, but the clergy had selected them and appointed them to Littlewood's command when he'd been charged with his new duties. Here in the New World, the local church authorities had deemed it necessary to establish an army of their own—small as it was—whose sole purpose lay in the discovery and destruction of witches. Littlewood was a God-fearing man and took his duties seriously, but he did not approve of the violence his subordinates reveled in. He did not like violence against women. Mostly, he did not care to see anyone mistreated before they'd had a trial. His father had been hung unjustly, and the memory of that innocent man swinging haunted Littlewood's dreams. That very act had prompted Littlewood's mother to leave England and come to the New World. Seeing his father's accusers delight in his death had sown a seed for justice deep in Littlewood's heart, which in turn had led him to the army here in the colonies and prompted him to join the Revolution.

More than anything, Littlewood wanted freedom and justice for all. Hadn't he seen to it that the witch, one Alison Delaney, had been given the best treatment afforded a prisoner while awaiting her trial? Well, he had done the best he could do for a witch, anyway. He had put an end to the abuse she suffered at the hands of his subordinates as quickly as possible.

It was Littlewood's task to track the rumors of witches, to hunt them, to bring them in; but he was no judge. Judgment was in the hands of God and therefore in the hands of the clergy. The clergy in this case was Reverend Mitchell. Mitchell had insisted on Delaney's execution.

Littlewood did not love executions. The murder of his father had fouled his taste for such things. But he knew that evil must be put away from the land. Witchcraft must be eradicated. Those who deal with the devil and with his minions must be cleansed with fire and removed from the world if the good people of the colonies were to prosper. It was Littlewood's duty, and a part of him despised it.

For that purpose—and that purpose alone—Littlewood was thankful to have Dobbs and McCutcheon. They would do the dirty work and do it gladly. Littlewood had never had to drag a woman to the pyre, never had to bind her to the stake. Not once had he had to light the fire himself. There were always locals who volunteered, eager and yearning to do their part for the Kingdom of Heaven and for the greater good of the people in their villages and towns.

This ramshackle hamlet in the middle of a backwater province was no exception. One of the local men, a chandler named Edmund Bell, had come forward and offered to carry the torch. There was a fire in his eyes long before the torch was passed into his hands. Now the chandler stood by, waiting, as they all were waiting, for the reverend to pronounce his final judgment and give the order.

Littlewood gazed around the meager village, at the excited faces of these simple people, their small houses and large walls. He considered the big oak at the center of the square, not far from where the witch stood atop the cone-shaped pyre of stacked kindling. Doubtless much of the wood stacked beneath the witch's feet had fallen from that mighty tree. Littlewood imagined that tree had hosted its share of executions. People loved an execution. It broke up the monotony of their lives, took them away from the fields, got the women out of the house, taught the children the valuable lesson of justice done to those who are different, those who live outside the accepted norms.

Those gathered nearest to the pyre were the witch's accusers: a farmer named George Cartwright and his wife, who Littlewood believed was called Martha. There had been others who had come forward to give testimony at this woman's suggestion, but she had been the first, the most dominant, the most vocal. Her voice had been the fiercest, most ferocious in the crowd, hurling the cruelest of insults at the witch along with the litany of accusations. She had been the loudest, by far, and the most hateful; but she had not been alone. There were many others. There were always many lined up to point long fingers in the direction of an accused witch. Their names did not matter to Littlewood. He rarely bothered to learn names. Once his business was through and this witch was dead, he would move along to the next land, listen for rumors, and investigate another witch. He would not pass through these parts again. Often, once a witch was dealt with and crops bloomed fully to harvest, the children stopped vanishing and babies survived through the pregnancies and were born healthy, a single execution would satisfy a small society.

Finally, a cool wind blew in from the east, bringing with it the first rays of sunlight on the distant horizon. On cue, Reverend Mitchell spoke, his baritone voice rising clear into the chill November morn.

"Alison Delaney, you stand accused and convicted of witchcraft, of consorting with the devil himself. You are hereby sentenced to die by fire, having your sins forever cleansed. May the Lord have mercy on your soul."

"Same to you, preacher," said the bound woman. Her voice was strong, filled with hate and resentment; yet tinged with sincerity and sorrow. Something was lacking. Something that should have been there but was missing. Littlewood could not think of what it was. Her eyes darted from each of them in turn, the other soldiers, the chandler with the lighted torch, her accusers, and the morbid gathering of spectators, flitting past the reverend and lingering just long enough on Littlewood's eyes to send a piercing shiver to the center of his heart. "May God be merciful to every one of you."

Captain Littlewood dragged his reluctant gaze from the intrepid witch—that was it, he realized; it was fear. Fear was lacking from her voice, from her face. This woman faced death stoically, calmly. She was ready to go. An aching doubt began to creep into Littlewood's mind, but he shut it out and looked to the reverend. The preacher nodded; a single terse movement, his hoary head jerking down, then up.

"Light it," Littlewood told his men.

In unison, Dobbs and McCutcheon stepped forward, each angling for the edges of the pyre as Edmund Bell strode forward with purpose in his steps, the three of them aiming to set their blazing torches to the base of kindling piled beneath the feet of Alison Delaney.

As the men approached, Littlewood heard the witch breathe a soft chant in an unknown tongue, a whisper in the wind, a barely audible cadence of repeated syllables. He watched her closely, wondering if she was casting a spell over the men or praying to her gods.

Suddenly, she laughed, and turning her eyes upon the torchbearers one-by-one, the witch blew a small puff of air at each one. Each torch diminished, as if her breath had caught the flames and repressed them, then each firebrand rose to life once more, rising high and dancing in the twilight.

She lifted her face to the pale, pink sky and resumed whispering. Captain Littlewood could not make out her words. There was a peculiar feeling on his skin, tingling just below the surface, creeping up his spine. Something cold touched the tips of his ears, his nose, the exposed flesh on the backs of his hands.

Snow.

Dark clouds were converging in the previously clear sky, gathering above the town square, centering above the stake to which the witch was bound. Swirling snow fell softly, carried on a cold wind. In an instant, the trio of torches were snuffed out, leaving behind slowly coiling trails of smoke where a moment before flames had danced in the morning gloom.

"She's a witch, for certain," said Edmund Bell, gasping. The chandler took a step back, his knuckles growing white as his grip tightened on the handle of the torch. "She speaks to the wind."

"You can speak to anything," said Alison Delaney, smirking, cool eyes narrowed and set upon the chandler, "if you know its name." She gazed from one torchbearer to another, grinning mischievously at the cold brands held in their hands, her attention making its way back to Edmund Bell in the end. "Do you know the flame's name, Edmund? Little Sylvia knows, doesn't she?"

Bell's face paled to the shade of the snow now falling in heavy swirling sheets about the square. He paused, then carefully drew out a small block of flint and a stick of steel. Crouching, quaking, not taking his eyes from the witch, Bell struck the steel to the flint, working to relight his torch.

"Who is Sylvia?" Littlewood asked.

"My daughter," Bell said, stuttering even as his hands trembled.

"How does she know your daughter's name?" Captain

Poorly Executed

Littlewood eyed the chandler suspiciously. He turned his gaze on each of the accusers, to the preacher, to the sullen-faced men of the town, and back to the chandler. A small knot of uneasy doubt twisted in his mind—the same doubt seemed to sit like a cyst on his conscience at each execution.

"She came to tend to her." Bell licked his lips. A spark jumped from the flint onto the oil-soaked cloth and the torch came to life. "To Sylvia, after she'd burned herself on the hearth."

"She came here a lot in the past," said George Cartwright, "before it was known she's a witch."

"Came to tend the ill," said a woman from the crowd. Something akin to the ache in Littlewood's mind seemed to hover on the woman's tongue. Pity? Sorrow? Doubt?

"I came to tend to many needs," said Alison Delaney. "To do many things."

Littlewood followed Alison's eyes to where she stared intently at George Cartwright and his wife. George turned away, casting his eyes down, a strange flush of red spreading over his neck and face. Perhaps Alison Delaney had tended to Mr. Cartwright's needs a time too many. The man's wife stared with open hatred at the pretty young woman bound upon the pyre.

A picture was forming in the captain's mind, a story unfolding. It was a familiar parable, one he had encountered many times—oh, so many times—though no one ever spoke the words of the tale aloud. He had felt a similar suspicion before, on several occasions. It was a situation that had made him doubt, at times, whether he truly believed in witches.

On one hand, he had to believe. His career was to hunt witches, to bring them to the local clergy for trial and judgment. It was his mission, his duty, his life's work. But on the other hand, he had never seen a witch work the magic she was said to possess. He had never witnessed anything that proved these women were in league with the devil. It was a dichotomy of beliefs, and a contradiction within him. Littlewood both believed and disbelieved in witchcraft.

But what of this woman? What of Alison Delaney, who stood before him now, strapped to a pole in the midst of encroaching flames? Was she truly a witch? Littlewood could not say. For so long he had questioned what he knew about witchcraft and magic, about demons and angels. God was God, Littlewood had little doubt of that; but aside from the divinity and authority of the Creator, Littlewood put little thought into the mechanics of the world and had less concern for spiritual affairs beyond his understanding. His calling was not to judge, nor to discern the truth of things. That's what the church leaders were for. Littlewood's job was to track witches and perform executions on behalf of local authorities and in the service of the clergy.

But did he really believe in witches? Perhaps.

Did he believe Alison Delaney possessed some power that gave her control over nature? Could she curdle milk in a cow's udder? Lay blight upon fields? Steal life from babies still in their mothers' wombs? Did this young woman with full red lips and big blue eyes have the ability to influence or control the minds of others? Probably not more than any other pretty girl who held that same power over men.

Edmund Bell stepped boldly toward the pyre and, without hesitation, plunged the burning torch into the haphazardly stacked kindling at the woman's feet. At first there was only smoke, which rose lazily to obscure Alison Delaney's pretty face and the wan, sad smile she now wore, as if resigned to this fate. The weak wood of the pyre was hesitant to catch, but after a moment, small reluctant flames began to spread. There came the sounds of crackling and popping, and Littlewood felt a rush of warmth surge toward him through the snowy breeze. It was comfortable and welcome, this new heat. He took another step forward, toward the slowly-building fire's embrace. Gradually, the warmth began chasing his chill away.

Captain Littlewood looked at her now, wondering. His doubt was increasing, but he fought to subdue it, to bury his misgiving under the weight of his duty. Smoke and flames stung his eyes. He glanced back at the farmer and his wife, saw George Cartwright's drawn face, downcast eyes, and the hard, cruel gaze of Martha Cartwright as she stared ahead at the helpless young woman bound at the center of the ring of flames. The suspicion within him was growing. He thought he knew precisely what spell Alison Delaney had cast over this community, over its dissatisfied men. He pitied her then, thinking she was innocent. Just a lonely young girl living in the wilderness, beyond the walls of the village, making her home and life in the forest and travelling into town to trade. He doubted she had done anything that deserved the death that was burning slowly toward her. It was too late to help. Too late to save her. Judgment had been rendered; the sentence executed.

The flames were nearly upon her.

Littlewood braced himself for the woman's cries. Nothing was worse than the lingering screams and searing scent of a burning witch. He expected weeping, wailing. This was not his first witch. Nor his first burning. They always cried out. Always begged for mercy. Crying out to the God they were accused of forsaking.

The flames were at her feet, but no sound came from Alison Delaney. No whimpering, no cursing. It was at this point they usually began to shriek. Littlewood stepped back from the fire, preparing himself for the stench of searing flesh to overcome the aroma of burning hickory and cherry.

He heard it then, the still soft voice from within the flames. Just under the voice of the praying reverend and the whipping wind, Littlewood could make out the gentle murmur of hushed words from the center of the smoking pyre.

Alison Delaney was speaking to the wild, calling softly to the snow.

Around him, Littlewood felt the wind pick up. The snow was falling now in heavy flakes, pushing down on the gathered crowd like a thick, wet membrane. Driven by the sudden gale, the blanket of snow obscured much of Littlewood's vision. It was becoming difficult for him to see anything clearly. Small swirling dust devils rose from the ground, like little snow-infused tornados, and strolled into the open flames, fighting to overcome the fire.

Littlewood's heart turned as icy as the air around him. He watched the writhing flames still, stop, and stand frozen in place. The flames diminished, fading to nothing, leaving behind ash and smoke, obscuring Littlewood's vision completely for the moment, and hiding the now-laughing Alison Delaney from his sight.

Part 2: Captured

The wind rose, the snow fell, and the gathered townspeople fell silent as the torches were plunged into the kindling. A great collective gasp echoed across the dawn as the flames layered upon themselves, rising bright and yellow into the early morning gloom. They wanted to look away then, Alison knew, but not one of them was able to pull their eyes away. There is something inherently intriguing in the agony of others. These good people were waiting for the song of her screams and the dance of her bound body upon the wreath of fire as her tired legs sprang into action trying to scrabble away from the encroaching inferno.

Her legs were weary from standing. Her mind and body ached from the long night's imprisonment in the little cage the soldiers had crammed her into. She was bloodied and bruised from where the two men had beaten her about her head and torso, pushing her down into the mud and kicking her with their heavy boots, spitting on her, cursing at her, fondling her breasts and buttocks even as they dragged her by her hair. The other man, the one they called Captain, had scolded them for this abuse, berated them, and had finally put an end to her torture by locking her inside the small cage at the edge of town.

She had lain like that, inclined, not enough room to lie down or stretch out, cramped up into a box the size of a cask until the preacher had come in the dark of night to weigh her against the duck. An absurd thing, but the best these simple people had. No logic in it. No truth. They had bound her to one side of a scale and set a live, flapping duck on the other plate. The counterbalance had not budged. Alison had weighed more than the little waterfowl. This had been enough to convict her of poisoning the well, plaguing the crops, lying with beasts, and selling herself wholesale to the prince of darkness.

And they called *her* a heathen.

She had never done any of the things of which she had been accused. No, they had never raised allegations for the one crime for which they were putting her to death. Alison had given herself to some of the (married) townsmen in exchange for goods. That, in itself, was a crime these Christian men would stone her for; but then they would have to stone the men as well, wouldn't they? And none of the women wanted to make public the knowledge their husbands had so readily turned to fornication—nay, adultery—seeking the beauty of a young outsider over the pudgy, aged familiarity of wives they had used up long ago. No. None of them wanted to suggest that Alison was preferable in the eyes of their men. Nor would they like it made known that these good, charitable men they had married had refused trading with a simple forest-dwelling woman and had instead lowered themselves to whoremongering, taking flesh for trade in lieu of merchandise.

It had not bothered Alison, these base, carnal acts. Not in the least. The deeds were natural, consensual, and simply part of the bartering process. Did not the wives of these men do the same thing, trading their flesh and sexual acts for the comfort and protection provided them by men? She had left each transaction without the items she'd brought to trade and with the goods she had come seeking. By her estimation, she was a shrewd businesswoman. She'd come trading for milk and eggs, offering the nuts and berries found near her home, the furs she'd taken from the rabbits and beavers she'd trapped. But the men of this settlement had no interest in what she offered, and one-by-one they had made their counteroffers.

The women had surmised the situation quickly. Within a fortnight, two children had died outside the village, dragged away by wolves or the like. Another had fallen ill, and two had been stillborn. The water in the well had soured. The harvest had gone poorly. Of course, Alison Delaney had

had nothing to do with any of those occurrences; but ample reason was supplied to the simple-minded, superstitious people of this hamlet and the witch hunters had been summoned.

They had come for her in the evening, as the sun began its descent beyond the curve of the world. In the twilight they came to her little shack, the one-room home built by Alison's mother when she had been forced into the wild, to survive on her own, cast away from a similar settlement. She had been a simple woman, in tune with nature, and had had a penchant for the healing arts using herbs and roots, applying unguents and ointments with strong, kind, gentle hands. She had not attended the church meetings, nor did she kneel in prayer; and so, she had been driven from society, left in the wild to trade with the townsfolk—the men—in the same manner in which they did business with Alison.

Alison's mother had been hanged for theft when Alison was still young enough to feel abandoned, yet just old enough to tend to herself in the tiny one-room shack in the heart of the forest. For two decades, Alison lived alone in the wild, gathering supplies, trapping animals, making and mending her own clothes; she travelled to the nearby towns and villages only when she thought it necessary, when she needed things she could not make for herself. Often, she would seek out those in need of medical help and, using the skills she had learned from her mother, would tend to the ill and the injured.

Poorly Executed

Along the way, she had met many men, though she'd been careful to not love any of them. Falling in love with a man could put an end to the life she knew, her life of solitude and freedom. She could not say the same for them, however, for men are fickle, lustful creatures and with an upturn of her full lips, a tilt in her flared hips, a soft touch or sultry whisper, many men had stumbled into her charms throughout the years. She hadn't set out to seduce anyone. That was not her goal. What Alison had intended was that level of flirtation that shades the realm between innocence and hope, where men become easily swayed; what she'd wanted was to trade and to receive fair prices for her goods. What she got, time and again, was a lusty man with a penchant for a pretty young girl he could send away when he'd gotten what he wanted from her.

She had known it would catch up to her someday. It had taken longer than she had expected. When they had come for her, this holy man and his soldiers—trembling boys who called themselves witch hunters—they'd already formed their opinions of her. Each of them had, in their doubtful, small minds and frail, fearful hearts, built up an image of the hag who dwelt in the depths of the woods. They had heard the tales from the locals of her power to entrance, enthrall and ensnare; of her powers and prowess and of the magic coursing through her, the plague of witchcraft spreading through the land at her command, cursing, manipulating, destroying all she put her mind to ruining, whether man, beast, or crop.

If any of her executioners knew the truth, they might take a moment to be ashamed of themselves. But they would not ask for it, she knew. None of these decent God-fearing men were here seeking the truth. Not one of them wanted to hear that she had never cast a spell, made a pact with demons, nor communicated with evil spirits. She had most certainly never sold herself to the devil, nor entertained any of his foul cohorts.

She was not a witch. Not in the sense these men thought of witches. Alison was a simple woman living her life as best she could, seeking to be at peace with the natural world around her. For the most part, she had gotten along fine on her own, living in her little home in the woods. On occasion she came into the villages and settlement to trade, to give or receive aid. The men of these places—these Puritan men, these God-fearing men—had bartered with her for her body, and Alison had given them what they wanted in exchange for what she needed. It was wrong. She knew it, and they knew. It probably should have never happened and would not have happened had not the men—every single one of the men—rudely, forcefully, lasciviously suggested that Alison put her body, her sexuality, in the bartering pool.

It did not matter now, though, did it? She was here, bloodied and in bonds, tied to a pillar of wood atop a burning pyre. She had taken a moment to pray, to ask God (for yes, she did believe) to help her. The man in charge, the one they called Captain, had watched her with a strange glint in his eye as Alison whispered her prayer into the wind. She had heard the gasps and cries of alarm when snow began falling and the wind whipped the flames from the shoddily crafted torches. They thought she had called to the wind, and perhaps she had; but most interesting was the fact that they seemed to believe the wind had come to her when she called.

Perhaps the wind had answered her. It could be they were right, that Alison Delaney held power within her of which even she was unaware. Her mother had taught her many things in the early days; had told her many stories. Alison knew the names of all the wild things: trees, shrubs, herbs, flowers, and each animal of the fields and forests, every fish in the lakes and streams. She knew the insects that lived in the trees, and in the dirt, and those that consumed the dead. Before she had learned to skin a rabbit, Alison had known the names of flames and rain, what snow was called when it fell as heavily as it was falling now. She knew the names of the east winds and the west, the north and south, and yes, often she did speak with them even as she spoke to her mother's spirit, the turtles and frogs, squirrels and dogs, the mist on the ground and the gas in the bog. She spoke to each of them even as she spoke to God.

Alison spoke to things she could feel and see, touch and taste and hear. For this, people branded her a witch. Yet when men and women talked with God, it was considered a holy, solemn, spiritual thing. But is God separate from the world he created? Was he not the still, small voice in the wind? The laughter of the waterfall? The rhythm and beauty in the hart's gait?

It did not matter. They were not burning her for speaking with God, though they had done that once, long ago, to a girl named Joan in a faraway land. Or so Alison's mother had once told her. Alison had not understood why men would kill a girl for praying, nor why her mother had told her of it. As Edmund Bell stepped forward with his newly lighted torch, Alison was thankful her mother had told her that tale, had tried to prepare her for such a time as this.

She held the chandler in her gaze. There was nothing left to say. She had spoken her piece and was ready to die with dignity.

Edmund Bell mustered his courage and lurched forward, driving his torch into the oil-drenched pyre beneath Alison Delaney. The wood caught quickly, crackling and smoking. Tears sprang to her eyes. Not from fear, nor from despair, but from the stinging of smoke and ash.

In all her years of isolation, Alison had never felt so alone.

These people did not know her. Not really. Not in the way one longs to be known by another. Not one of them knew Alison deeply, intimately, though they had known her all her life. Had known her as a young girl and watched her grow, coming and going as she did from their town, from their lives. Oh, yes, they knew her well enough, if not half as well as they should. And they certainly knew she was no witch.

Poorly Executed

If she had possessed the powers they feared, they wouldn't have come for her. If she could call fire and snow, lightning, and beasts, would she not have done so and set herself free? Could she keep her mind filled with these questions and ignore the pain of the flames as they crawled upon her flesh?

This fire was damned hot. Something would have to be done about that. She wasn't really going to die this way, was she? But what was she supposed to do about it? Blow the flames out? Perhaps that wasn't such an absurd idea. It could not hurt to try.

What if she was the witch they accused her of being? What if she had the power they claimed she had? Could it be that people had been right about her all along and she had never known? No time like burning alive to discover yourself, she thought wryly.

Either I'm a witch, or I'm not. One way to find out, and it does not involve a duck or a scale.

Alison pulled in a deep breath and blew out with all her strength. A strong gust of wind rushed in from the east, driving a blinding fury of thick snow before it.

"She calls to the wind!" someone shouted.

Huh. I'm calling. Some rain would be nice, too.

The flames were upon her, creeping in close and rising high. The ropes that bound her hands were growing hot. If she was a witch, truly, the way these people feared, she would break these bindings, summon a storm, and leap from this pyre.

230

Her hands, benumbed and cold from being suspended above her, twisted and writhed against the heat of the fire and suddenly there was a weakening, a give, and the twine broke. Alison pulled her hands free in a powerful, jerking motion and they fell heavily to her sides. There was no circulation in her hands, no feeling; just numbness from being held for so long in such an unnatural position.

The weight of the snow increased.

The wind ripped through the flames.

Rain began falling.

Part 3: Hanging in the Rain

Louis Littlewood could not believe what he was seeing. In all his years, he had never witnessed the magical powers of a witch. He had always doubted. Always. Of course, he had wanted to believe, wanted to know he was doing the right thing, doing God's will. There was the constant need to justify the actions of his duty. So often, he had feared he was murdering women simply on men's orders; but now he knew, now he saw with his own eyes and heard with his own ears that a witch could call on the strength of God's creation to serve her will.

The fire was out. Smoke filled the square. Panic was erupting about him and his men were either cowering or standing slack-jawed: useless, the lot of them. But Littlewood's resolve was renewed. He knew what he must do.

Poorly Executed

The witch leapt from the pyre and broke into a sprint, heading for the edge of the village, her bare feet pounding the muddy, snow-covered ground. Through the snow and rain and smoke, Littlewood knew he could lose track of her quickly.

"Dobbs," Littlewood cried. "McCutcheon. After her. You men there, cut her off."

Half the men obeyed his command. It was more than he had expected. In the face of true witchcraft, just how much courage could he count on?

It was Edmund Bell who got to her first, hurling himself through the storm and tackling the petite woman. The chandler grunted. The witch cried out, her voice high and frightened. A pang of sympathy ran through Littlewood like a sad song pealing across the pale morn, for he knew the woman was hurt and afraid. He squashed his pity. Pity was for the innocent. For people. Not for demons. Nor for the devil's consorts. Still, he wanted desperately for this to be done.

The other men surrounded the tangled bodies of Bell and the woman, but none would approach. Their fear kept them at bay.

"Well done, you lot," said Littlewood, sarcasm dripping from each word. "Up, you," he said, taking the small woman by her soiled ginger hair and pulling her savagely to her feet. He half-dragged, half-led the woman back toward the pyre, not sure of what his plan was but certain he needed to put her down swiftly.

What to do? You are supposed to burn a witch. That's what he had always been told. In the distant past, it seemed they used to stone them; but stoning seemed messy, and it was too cold, too snowy to search for stones.

Littlewood forced the witch to her knees, still gripping her hair tightly in one hand. She struggled and groaned, her small hands grasping at his, clawing, working to peel his fingers loose. He was too strong for her, too focused. He gave her hair a savage twist, yanking some loose from the scalp. She squealed and subsided.

"What do we do now?" McCutcheon asked from a dozen feet away. His eyes were darting from the witch to the smoking mound of half-charred wood. He was shivering in the wind, his red coattails flapping like unfurled sails caught in a squall.

"Can't burn her," Dobbs offered. "That was poorly executed. The fire I mean. She was ready for that."

"But what else can we do?" McCutcheon asked. "You're supposed to burn a witch. Everyone knows that."

"Aye," said Dobbs, nodding sagely. "Everyone knows."

"Reverend?" Littlewood called through the din of rain and wind. "Reverend Mitchell?"

"Yes," came a distant call. "I'm here."

A black-garbed figure appeared amid the swirling snow. He could not have been more than thirty paces from where Littlewood stood, but he was nothing more than an obscured image in that storm.

"What other methods can kill a witch?" Littlewood

shouted.

Again, the woman struggled, this time striking out and punching Littlewood in the groin. The pain caught him off-guard, and the witch sprang to her feet, pouncing catlike between Dobbs and McCutcheon. The pair froze, allowing her to dash past them.

"Grab her, you fools," Littlewood barked.

McCutcheon, who was by far the larger of the two men, stepped after Alison Delaney, his stride easily gaining on her, the long reach of his arm grabbing her by the wrist and pulling her to him as if the two were not predator and prey but instead dance partners in a snow globe. He caught her in his arms, face to face, her beautiful blue eyes peering into his with that mixture of fear and hate coupled with a frantic plea for mercy that only a victim can muster, and that she can only assemble for her assailant.

"Oh, to hell with this," McCutcheon said, pushing her suddenly, violently away from himself.

Alison Delaney was reeled into McCutcheon's grip and twirled into Dobbs' arms so quickly, she looked to Littlewood like a graceful dancer.

"Oh no," said Dobbs. "No, no, no. I've had enough of this." He pushed the woman roughly down, so she was on all fours before him. As she straightened, gathering her legs beneath her to pounce and flee once more, Dobbs swung his musket from his shoulder and put it against the back of her head.

"You carry that loaded?" McCutcheon asked, dubious.

"When witches are about," said Dobbs, the implication in his voice was that McCutcheon had asked a stupid question.

"You cannot shoot her," said the reverend.

"The hell I can't," Dobbs called over his shoulder. "A bullet in the brain'll put her down, sure enough."

"It won't cleanse her."

"Not my job," Dobbs said. "You talk to the boss about that—God, I mean. I just put 'em down."

"Stand down, Dobbs," Littlewood said.

On her knees, hands raised halfway to the sky, eyes shifting about the hazy village, Alison Delaney drew in a long, shuddering breath.

"What can we do, preacher?" Littlewood asked, impatience sullying his tone. "This has gone on long enough."

"You can hang her. There. From the old oak at town's center."

"No!" the woman cried. "No." She was weeping and frantically trying to crawl away.

"Shut your mouth." Dobbs pushed her face into the mud with the butt of his musket. "Help me get her up," he said to McCutcheon. "You, Bell, get us some rope."

"How much?" asked the chandler.

"Enough to hang a witch." Dobbs looked at McCutcheon, then to Captain Littlewood, his expression asking them, *can you believe this?*

"No," said the witch again, as they pulled her to her

bruised and bloodied feet. "They hanged my mother. I don't want to die that way."

"Nobody wants to die any way," said McCutcheon. "Nobody gets a say in it."

They marched her to the tree, dragging her, for, Littlewood reckoned, fear and resignation were vying for control within her. An unseen finger plucked a chord of pity on his heartstrings. He had never faced a hanging himself. Or any execution for that matter. Not from the side Alison was facing it now.

"Don't do this," she pleaded, sobbing. "Don't. Please."

"It'll be over soon enough," said Dobbs. "Stop struggling. It'll go easier for you."

"Hanging never goes easy," Alison said. "Not for anyone."

Edmund Bell emerged from the snow with a long coil of rope and sent a young boy scurrying up into the tree to throw one end over a thick branch. In the distance, beyond the town's palisades, lightning flashed. By the time the boy shimmied down the tree's trunk, the sound of thunder was rolling overhead.

"Alison Delaney," said the reverend. "You have been found guilty of witchcraft and of consorting with the devil. You are hereby sentenced to die by hanging."

"Please," she whimpered as a dark sac was forced over her head. "No."

"You have to go through the whole thing again?" Littlewood asked.

Reverend Mitchell ignored the captain. "May God have mercy on your soul." He drew out a small flask from a pocket in his black coat, uncorked it, and splashed some of the liquid within on the woman's head and body.

Mitchell nodded to Littlewood.

"Do it," Littlewood said.

Dobbs had finished fashioning the noose—a task Littlewood was surprised to see the man do with such ease, speed and skill—and deftly slipped it over the witch's head.

The three soldiers worked in unison, pulling the rope, hand-over-hand, the bough above groaning over the wind's harsh whistles as it took the full weight of Alison Delaney.

Hands hanging limping before her, face covered by the black hood, the accused witch was hoisted into the air, legs kicking. She squirmed a bit but made not a sound. There seemed to be no fight left in her now. If not for the quick, jerking movements of her twitching hands and shuddering body, Louis Littlewood would have thought the witch was finally quite dead.

Part 4: The Breaking of the Storm

Alison Delaney was not dead. Not yet.

She was not a praying woman in the Christian sense. There was no gathering with others in a musty church building once a week. No kneeling. No learning the ritualized chants and phrases, no practice of audible call-and-response. There was nature, and there most certainly was a God in nature—quite probably the very same God these townsfolk worshipped, in their own way. Though Alison did not self-flagellate or lie prostrate, she did often commune with nature, call out to God, speak to the spirit from beyond, whatever name people wished to put upon it.

And now, as the twisting rope pulled taut around her throat, choking off air, blood and life, she prayed. Her words were ragged and stunted, truncated by the noose, diminished by the pain. Her legs kicked, searching for ground on which to stand, but found only empty air as she was lifted high, floating above the world like an angel, a spirit, a ghost; but she was none of these. She was a woman, a simple woman, and now she was the victim of murder. They were killing her, of that there was no doubt. But these men—her executioners—were not good at their job.

Oh, they had tracked her and captured her, dragged Alison back to their *civilized* society, stuffed her in a cage and put her on "trial" before the man in black; but their duty in killing her now was poorly executed. They had failed at burning her, believing she had somehow called on the wind and rain to rescue her from them, but perhaps these men had built a weak pyre. Mayhap, not knowing how to kindle a proper fire, they had used green wood. Perhaps they had stacked that green wood too close together; so close, in fact, that no air could flow between the branches to feed the flames. They had used oil (she had smelled it long before they had bound her to the post at the pyre's center), and the oil had caught and burned. Oil would light no matter the condition of the wood. The oil-fueled flames would slide upon the damp, green wood and, unable to catch properly, would eventually peter out.

These privileged men in their officer's uniforms had probably never lighted their own fires. Alison suspected they had underlings and subordinates, slaves, and servants, to do such things.

And now they had fashioned a makeshift, loose-fitting noose designed to strangle and choke, but seemed to be failing in the designated task. Though she felt as if she were dying, Alison doubted the discomfort from this chafing rope would actually kill her. The noose tightened and she was hoisted from the ground. Silently, Alison cried out to God as she clawed at the noose. It was no use. The ill-crafted noose was just tight enough that she could not get her fingers between the rope and her flesh.

Raising her hands above her, giving her legs and torso over to the squirming rhythm of the gallows dance, Alison croaked to the heavens, her gagging, rasping voice calling out for deliverance. Her neck was stretching miserably. She could feel the bruises forming. Her ears filled with the pulsing sound of the ocean as blood pumped rhythmically like a tide rising and falling.

Falling.

She was a simple woman, the kind of woman who lived at peace with the world around her, in harmony with the creatures and plants of the wild. She'd tried to maintain relations with the people of the nearby villages, but that had not been so easy for her. Though they'd treated her with disdain and indifference, she had never harbored any ill will toward any of them, whether European or native. Yet these people had formed some opinion of her, believing she hated them, hated their God; but there was no truth in those accusations. She did not disrespect them or their beliefs. In fact, she held many of them in esteem, respecting their endurance and perseverance in this new land.

Still, they distrusted her. They feared her. For a reason Alison had never known, had never understood, these people believed she was in league with devils and demons. They believed she was an enemy to them, an enemy of their God. They believed she was evil. She was not. Alison wanted to live in peace with them, yet be free to dwell as she saw fit, to be wild and free in the land she called home. She was a simple woman with simple desires. Alison Delaney simply did not possess the powers of witchcraft these people believed she possessed. She could not call curses. She could not control the weather, bring plagues, change forms, and she did not commune with evil spirits.

Yet, as she dangled despairingly from a low branch of a tall oak, her weakened body jerking and dancing like a flag in the wind, she called out to God. Called out to whatever forces of nature might be listening and might be willing to come to her and deliver her from this horrible fate.

And as she prayed, something happened.

The heavy snow subsided, clearing the sky and letting the fresh bright morning burst through. A fierce wind stirred around her, spinning her, at the end of her rope, round and round like a weathervane. Above her, a sound like a volley of musket shots broke through the early daylight, flooding into her pulsating ears as if from far away.

Another crack sounded in the sky above her. The world shifted weirdly. She was losing consciousness, slowly. Her soul was rising, lifting out of her. She was not ready to die. With all her strength, Alison drew in a shuddering breath and with that breath she reeled in her departing spirit. She could feel her soul slipping in and out, pulling away. Ebbing. Rising. Rising slowly away from her body.

She tried to hold onto it. Reached for her spirit with both hands upturned, grasping, taking hold on nothing. Then came a sound like ice cracking in spring's first melt. The world spun once more and the noose came loose, so loose, and Alison felt her soul sliding back into place, descending...falling.

Falling so fast.

It was a long fall back to earth for Alison Delaney and for her fleeing spirit, but falling they were. Plummeting.

But she was not dead. Not yet.

As the first full breath filled her burning lungs, Alison realized she had never felt so full of life. As she plunged toward the earth from which she'd come, Alison was filled with an energy she had never felt before.

She knew, in that moment, her prayer had been answered.

Poorly Executed

Part 5: A Shot in the Head

The tree branch broke. The witch fell. Her body struck the frozen earth with a hollow thud. She was writhing and twisting, but still living.

"Enough of this," Littlewood said, his shaky voice betraying his fear. "Get her on her knees."

Dobbs and McCutcheon wasted no time grabbing the witch before she could compose herself. They had seen what Littlewood had seen. She had used her power to clear away the snow and snap the branch from which she hung. What manner of woman had the power to break the limb of an oak that size? A witch, Littlewood knew. A witch could do such things.

To hell with the reverend and the church laws. They had tried twice to kill her by orthodox standards and both attempts had been poorly executed. It was time to end this.

The soldiers forced the witch to her knees in the snow and mud, each holding an arm, and Littlewood put the barrel of his musket against the back of her head.

"God grant you mercy," Littlewood said, and he shot the witch in her head.

Part 6: Freedom in the Flight

Alison struck the ground, hard. Something in her broke and she cried out. Something else, deeper, broke loose and was rising to the surface of her mind. A great power, a fury, buried deep. A force, ancient and powerful, was welling in her like a spring of living water and filling her with a strength she had never known before.

She tried to right herself, to pull the rope from her neck and get to her knees.

"Enough of this," said a deep voice from beyond the veil of her senses. "Get her on her knees."

What did it mean? Alison could make no sense of it. Before she could find her bearings, rough hands seized her, and she was being dragged once again across the sloppy cold ground. She was set on her knees, the heels of her feet pressing painfully into her buttocks. Her arms were yanked back at the elbows, her spine was forced erect in that age-old posture of submission.

Something cold and hard was pressed against the back of her skull.

Her vision suddenly cleared. All her senses came alive. She heard the hammer of the musket lock into place. Saw the black-garbed preacher moving in slow motion some distance away, his mouth locked in a small circle, caught on the last note of long, drawn-out "Noooooo". Smelled the powder in the barrel, the flint and steel, the charred remains of the dying embers, the freshness of the snow and rain. Felt on her skin the dew of the day, the tickle of the breeze, and beneath her flesh, the bruising, the blood rushing to its work, healing the trauma inflicted by these three brave men.

Behind her, she heard the telltale click of the trigger being squeezed, followed by the deafening boom of the musket backfiring, the barrel and haft snapping like the tree branch from which she had recently hung. There was a flash of light, bright and blinding and Alison felt her captors release her arms.

There was a dull ache in the back of her head. The smell of smoke was in her nostrils, fresh and near, closer than the pyre smoke that had surrounded her just minutes ago. It was pungent, scented of charcoal and sulfur, with a hint of aged urine. Gunsmoke. She knew what had happened, had seen it before when men were hunting. The gun had jammed and backfired.

The three soldiers recoiled, eyes and ears covered, blinded and deafened. The preacher and the chandler were turned away, shielding their eyes. All the townspeople stood stock still, sullen, surprised and silent. In all the world, Alison doubted anything was moving in that moment.

Deftly, she pulled the black sack from her head and pulled the noose away from her neck, loosening it enough to allow breath to be drawn. Leaping to her feet, she fled toward the town's gate. This was her chance. She had a moment's reprieve, a head start, and as she passed through that gate, she did not look back.

Alison fled, her feet beating the muddy path that served as a road to and from the little village where they had tried to kill her. What a magnificent effort on their part, for these men, her executioners, would not relent. They had tried three times to end her life and would try again, she knew, if only they could gather their wits and give chase. And chase her they would. Of this, Alison had no doubt.

As she fled, she was acutely aware of the sharp pain in her wrists and the weariness in her legs. Her hands were at last liberated of the bonds of the poor bindings, the coarse, burning, twisted twine that had been so forcefully looped about her slender wrists with such cruelty that the skin was raw and torn, bleeding and chafed. Alison had no recollection of freeing herself from those bindings, but she now moved with the easy grace of the unfettered, the renewed strength of a captive freed.

Her fingers leapt to her neck. There they searched until they found hold on the noose still dangling haphazardly like an adornment. Repulsed by it, anguished by the memory of her mother's kicking corpse swinging and spinning, terrified by the recent torment that noose had caused her, Alison tore it away, yanking it up and over her red-crowned head and casting it away, thrusting it fiercely from her and out into the rising daylight.

Her necked ached terribly. There was fire rushing through her brain. Her feet pushed wildly at the ground, driving her onward into the unknown wild—a wilderness that should have been known to her but was now strange and distorted, as if her homeland woodland were a foreign place, a realm of shadow and mystery that should have been familiar in this clear light of early morning. In her chest, her heart leapt, bounding from rib to rib, swelling, trying to push its way out of her mouth, through her chest. Her mouth was dry. So dry. Yet her feet did not stop churning.

Poorly Executed

She was heading home, home to where she had spent all her days, where her mother had raised her and taught her the ways of the world, the wild world, the world she now felt akin with, attuned to.

As she sprinted from the land of civilization and returned to the wilderness from whence she'd come, Alison remembered her youth in these woods, the festivals and celebrations she'd shared with her mother. They had celebrated the solstices and equinoxes, the new moons and the full. There had been a time when Alison had been one with the forest, a chamber in the beating heart of the wild. She had believed herself one with nature still; her capture the day before could not change that. Yet, it seemed so long ago, so far away in the stream of time, as if the years, days, and seasons drew out in a long, winding road that led into the infinite past. Alison felt as if she had been disconnected from her own life and was now, here on this unfamiliar path, with the coldness of winter enveloping her, the snow beneath her feet pulling her down into a deep freeze, only beginning to once again feel the touch of the magic of the world.

Yes, there was magic. It was all around her, in the trees, in the air, in the creatures of the forest. There was magic in their names. Flame. Star. Tree. Deer. Each had its own power, as Alison had hers. She could feel it now, welling up within her, a fierce glow of warm light burning from within. And inner strength that coursed through her like blood.

She was suddenly in full possession of all her senses,

each heightened, keen, and she found herself altogether alert. The burning, the hanging, the beating, the shooting: something in the horrible disturbance of her physical being had awoken a dormant power within and now Alison Delaney could sense, feel, observe everything…every single thing. She heard the owl call and the hawk answer, the pitter patter of the hopping feet of the hare fleeing both; the soft disturbance in the air as each snowflake fell. Alison felt the touch of each drop of water form as that snow melted upon her warm flesh, tickling her nose, cheeks, the tips of her ears. She could hear the creaking of the trees as they chilled and swayed and was able to discern which cracking or groaning belonged to each; yes, Alison could discern the sound of oak from maple, hickory from pine, now the shivering of a cedar and the trembling of an elm. Each of them sang and complained in a tongue she now heard clearly.

Her eyes saw far and near. Saw the needles of the pines, green and brown. Saw branches sagging gently beneath the new snow. Saw the veins in each leaf still struggling for life, and she knew death was imminent: it could be avoided just so long, but not robbed. She saw the foxes in their holes and the leaping deer at the stream's edge. Ah, the stream. Finally, a familiar sight. It was here she had gathered water, speaking with the twitchy white rabbits and watching the kind old brown bears lumber by. Now there were only the deer, two of them, drinking and watching Alison approach. Beneath the stones, insects milled about, digging, huddling, mating, waiting. Some were sleeping now, others eating. She could feel the movement beneath her feet of all the earth-dwellers going about their business and she smiled, knowing that she was home at last, back home in a world that made sense, a world where all things lived as they were made to live. A world yet untouched by the superstitious hands of men.

She came to the stream, a trickle of water in the heart of the forest that she knew well. A single fish slid downstream, pushing against the current, then was followed by its school, as if they had been waiting for the scout to make safe the passage. She had taken fish from this stream. Possibly she'd eaten this one's ancestors. Part of her felt ashamed of that.

No time now to linger. Alison focused her attention on the land behind her, listening and watching for pursuers. She saw no men, though she sensed them nearby. There were voices, though, in the distance. Far away words. Many men speaking to one another, laughing, jesting. There was no shouting, no one crying out that they had discovered her. It was too much to hope for, but Alison had the impression that her executioners were finished with her.

They had had their fun, hadn't they? Now it seemed they were content to let her be.

Yet, she *felt* them. Felt their bodies near to hers, as if they were right here with her, above her, *on top* of her. Convulsively, Alison shuddered at that thought.

Near or far, it did not matter. Either way she needed to cross the stream. Her home lay just beyond. If she could get there, could reach home, maybe she could enact the magic she felt welling up within her, could call on the powers manifesting inside and hide herself from the world of men. They could not harm her again. Not now. They had done all they could to her. She just needed to cross over. To reach the other side. She was so close.

She put one foot into the whispering waters. The deer looked at her and, as one, they fled into the trees, vanishing. There came a flash of lightning. A burning, blinding light that consumed her vision and struck her like a thunderbolt. Her eyes clenched shut. Pain ripped through her. A sound of thunder deafened her, and Alison Delaney lurched forward, falling face first into the snow, her hands catching her in the muddy water.

Everything went dark. She pushed on, scrabbling, clawing, kicking. If she could just reach the other side.

She was nearly there. Alison was almost...

Part 7: Home

Littlewood squeezed the trigger.

The iron ball left the barrel, parted the back of Alison Delaney's hair, and tore into the witch's skull, bounced around in the grey matter for a moment, and finally exited through her left eye.

Dobbs and McCutcheon released her arms and let her fall, each leaping back.

She landed on all fours and, though Littlewood had little

doubt the bullet in the brain had done its work, the witch took three lurching steps forward on her trembling arms and twitching knees before collapsing face first into the cold mud and crisp snow.

After so much effort, and such a poor effort to burn her, and to hang her, Alison Delaney was finally dead.

"What have you done?" asked Reverend Mitchell, eyes wide, jaw hanging slack.

"Killed your witch," answered Littlewood.

"Not with a gunshot," said the reverend. "Never with a gunshot."

"Dead is dead," said Dobbs. "Don't see what the big deal is."

"Things are done a particular way for a reason," said the reverend.

"What would you have us do?" asked Littlewood. "Want us to raise her and kill her again?"

"Burn her," said the reverend. "At least burn the corpse."

"All right," said Littlewood. He looked at his men. "Burn her."

Dobbs and McCutcheon carried the brainless, lifeless body of the dead witch to the smoldering pyre and tossed her on the smoking remnants like a sack of grain being loaded on a cart.

"Light it," Littlewood ordered for the second time that day.

McCutcheon went to work soaking the body and the

wood with lamp oil. There was little chance the dead witch could fight the flames now.

Still, Edmund Bell came forward, torch lighted, and, reluctant now to approach the corpse of the witch, handed the firebrand over to Dobbs who took it and tossed it upon the body, sending the witch back to wherever it was she had come from.

"What now?" Dobbs said, looking at the captain.

"Now," said Littlewood, watching the pyre, basking in the warmth of the flames. "Now we can finally go home."

~~~

Notes on Poorly Executed

Our society and history are rife with tales of witch trials and executions.

We have movies, books, and a horrible history that speak volumes for the beliefs and lifestyles of people in early colonial America. Witch trials were real, absurd, brutal things. I wanted to write about the accusers, the accused, the witch hunters, the executioners, and how they saw each other. We never can be sure of what is transpiring in the minds of those around us, what their motives are, how they view us, what doubts linger in their minds. I wanted to get into the head of the "witch" and inside the minds of those responsible for bringing her to "justice."

About the Author

C. L. Phillips is the author of the collections *Figures in the Forest and other tales* and *A Candle in the Dark and other tales*. He writes from Michigan, where he plays a weekly Dungeons and Dragons session with his sons and friends. His stories have been included in multiple anthologies. Currently, there is another collection in the works, as well as a novel.

A lifelong lover of the written word, he spends his free time writing, reading, and delving into new worlds via video games. Visit amazon.com/author/c.l.phillips or follow him at cl-phillips.com for stories and information.

Made in the USA
Middletown, DE
24 October 2023

41332133R00146